Ida

MURDER SERVED HOT

The 5th Nikki Hunter Mystery

Nancy Skopin

3/29/16
To Ida,
Enjoy!
Nancy

Murder Served Hot
The Fifth Nikki Hunter Mystery

First Print Edition: March 2016

Cover and Formatting: Streetlight Graphics

These books could not be completed without an amazing team:

Editor – Juliann Stark

Proofreaders – Nicoli Baily & Max Ferry

Law Enforcement Consultant – Mark Pollio

Chapter 1

"I'd like to tell you a little bit about myself," Brooke Evans began, "so you'll understand the choices I've made."

"Okay," I said, already curious.

"I've always been attracted to bad boys. You know the type. Slightly dangerous, extremely macho, emotionally distant. Most of them are assholes. The last guy I dated was a major jerk. After we'd been seeing each other for a few months he tried to get me to have a three-way with him and another woman. We got back to his place after dinner one night and he said he had a surprise for me. There was a naked woman in his bed, waiting for us. She was really slutty-looking too. Probably a prostitute.

"I'd had a lot to drink, but I wasn't *that* drunk. I said no and tried to leave, but he wouldn't let me. He hit me in the face and threw me down on the bed. Then he made me watch while he screwed her. I guess he thought it would make me hot or something, but it was disgusting. I managed to get out the door and that was it for me. No more bad boys. I decided to look for someone nice. A month later I met Stanley. He's a CPA. He did my taxes. Who could be more harmless than an accountant, right?"

I was dumbfounded. I motioned for her to go on.

"Stanley and I have been dating for eleven months now, since March, and last week he asked me to marry him. I was kind of surprised because we've never even had sex. I think he's old fashioned, you know, and wants to wait until we're married. Anyway, ever since he proposed he's been acting really weird. He wants to know where I am all the time, my apartment has to be spotless, and he makes me get on the scale every time I see him. If I gain an ounce, or I'm even a minute late when we're going out, he gets upset.

"At first I thought it was kind of cute and quirky. But now I think maybe he has that obsessive compulsive thing. OCD? Stanley says 'You have to establish strict control over everything in your life in order to maintain balance.' I guess that kind of makes sense, but it's getting old, if you know what I mean. He makes me carry a pager, and I think he might be having me followed. He's a very sweet guy, but I'm beginning to think marrying him might be a mistake."

I'd never missed an episode of Monk, when it was on TV, and immediately flashed on the OCD Detective's relationship with his wife, Trudy. I was tempted to ask if Stanley ever kissed her or held her hand, but I didn't think it was any of my business at this point.

"So, what would you like me to do?" I asked.

"I want you to run a complete background check on me, and one on Stanley. If he checks up on me and finds out about my past, the kind of guys I dated before I met him, I think he'll flip. So I want to know if that kind of information is available. And I want you to follow me to see if I'm being followed by someone else. And I want you to follow Stanley."

"I usually work alone," I said. "If you want Stanley followed at the same time as I'm tailing you, I'll have to bring in an associate or two. This is going to be expensive."

“I have money. My parents passed away two years ago. They were very well off, and they had a huge life insurance policy. I was an only child.”

“Okay. I’ll need your social security number for the background report. And I’ll need Stanley’s driver’s license or social security number.”

Brooke took the notepad I handed her and wrote down her social security number. “I don’t know Stanley’s,” she said. “And I’ve never even seen his driver’s license. I can give you his date of birth and his address.”

She wrote the info on the notepad and handed it back to me. Stanley’s last name was Godard. “This is his home address,” she said, pointing to a line she’d written on the notepad, “And this is his office.”

“That’s a start. But try to get a look at his driver’s license for me. I can’t do a background check without either that or his social security number.”

Brooke was a strikingly beautiful woman in her early thirties. Aristocratic features, intelligent brown eyes, a radiant complexion, and lustrous brown hair with subtle blonde highlights. She had a well-toned body, which was evident because she was wearing shorts and a tank top. It was late February, but spring had hit the California coast early and it was already seventy-three degrees outside. Brooke also had a subtle drawl. The whole package brought to mind the quintessential Southern belle.

My name is Nicoli Hunter. I'm a private investigator licensed to practice in the state of California. My office is in Redwood City, in a marina complex where I also live aboard my forty-two foot Cheoy Lee Motorsailer, *Turning Point*. I've been a PI for almost three years now, not counting the two years I spent in training. I'm thirty-six, five foot seven, and a hundred and thirty-four pounds, with long chestnut-brown hair and dark blue eyes. I'm no slouch in the looks department, but Brooke almost made me feel plain.

"Do you have a photograph of Stanley?" I asked.

She withdrew her wallet from her Chloe shoulder bag and flipped it open. Removing a small picture from one of the compartments, she hesitated before giving it to me.

"Can you make a copy of this?" she asked. "It's the only one I have, and I'm afraid he'll notice if it's missing."

"He keeps track of what's in your wallet?" I asked.

She shrugged. "Maybe."

"I'll scan it," I said.

She handed over the photo and I slipped it into my color scanner. While I was running the scan application I told her my hourly rate.

"If I bring in another PI, I'll also be charging you for their time and expenses. I'll need a deposit to get things started."

I saved and printed the scanned picture and handed her the photo. Brooke slid the picture back into her wallet and took out her checkbook.

"How much do you need?" she asked.

I did some quick calculations in my head, adding up my time and that of a colleague, mileage, and the expense of the background checks.

"If you want someone to watch both you and Stanley twenty-four hours a day, the first week will cost you around thirty-four thousand. Twenty thousand if you only want to be followed during daylight hours."

"Can you follow me from when I get off work until, say, midnight? And watch Stanley during the day?"

"Sure."

She wrote me a check for thirty thousand

dollars and placed it on my desk blotter. I picked it up.

"Is this your current address?"

"Yes. My home phone number is on there too."

I filled in the blanks on my standard contract and printed two copies. Brooke didn't even read it before signing on the dotted line. I signed a copy and held it out to her.

"I can't take that," she said. "What if he finds it?"

"Brooke, this is none of my business, but if you're so nervous around Stanley, why are you still seeing him?"

"He's not a bad guy. He's just been a little strange since he proposed. Maybe the idea of marriage is stressing him out."

"Did you accept?"

"Excuse me?"

"Did you accept his proposal?"

"Oh. Not exactly. I said I wanted to think about it."

"Maybe that's what's stressing him out."

"You think?" she asked, hopefully.

"When are you going to see him again?"

"Tonight. We always go out on Friday night. Always to the same restaurant. The Garden Grill, in Menlo Park. Do you know it?"

I nodded. I knew the Garden Grill and its owner, Jessica James, quite well. Jessica and I had worked together years ago, when I was still in retail security management, and she was one of my first clients when I got my PI license.

"You go there every Friday?"

"Yes, and we always sit at the same table. Stanley likes routine."

"Which table?" I asked.

"The one in the tiny room with the glass ceiling, under the oak tree."

"Really? That's my favorite table too." Small world. "What time is your reservation?"

"Eight o'clock."

I asked Brooke where she worked and she said she was the Cosmetics Department Manager at the Stanford Neiman Marcus. She worked from 10:00 to 6:00, Monday through Friday. I wondered if she would let me use her employee's discount.

CHAPTER 2

AFTER BROOKE LEFT MY OFFICE I e-mailed her name and social security number to Criminal Investigative Services, asking for a complete background report, including financials and any criminal records in Santa Clara, San Mateo, San Francisco, and Alameda counties.

After sending the e-mail, I studied the scanned photo of Stanley Godard. In the picture he was seated behind a desk. He looked to be in his thirties, average weight, brown hair and eyes, with a half smile on his clean-shaven face. Not a bad looking guy, but the tension behind his soulful eyes was unmistakable.

I put in a call to Jim Sutherland, a fellow private investigator I'd met and befriended seven months ago when he was hired to follow me. Together we had apprehended the psycho killer who was, at the time, his client. Jim has a team of trained investigators working for him now, so when I need help he always manages to make time for me.

"Superior Investigations," said Jim's deep, resonant voice.

"You're answering your own phone? What's the world coming to?"

"Heather's out to lunch and everyone else is in the field. What's up Nikki?"

"I have a new client who wants surveillance on herself and her boyfriend."

"She thinks he's cheating, right?"

"No, she thinks he's gone a little bit nuts since he proposed. Wants to know if he's having her followed."

"Interesting. I assume this is a paying client."

The last job I'd needed Jim's help with had been for a nine-year-old boy whose mother had been murdered. Eventually the boy's uncle had paid me, and I'd paid Jim, but he'd accepted the job thinking it was a freebie.

"Absolutely. I have a check in my hand."

"Outstanding. You want me to tail the woman or the man?"

"I think you'll have more fun following her. She's a looker."

"You're too good to me."

"It's the least I can do. Can you get started tonight? They're having dinner at the Garden Grill at eight."

"Sure."

"I'll make us a reservation for seven-thirty and meet you there."

I hung up and called Bill Anderson, the Redwood City Police Detective I've been seeing steadily for the last seven months. Bill is a tantalizing mix of Irish and American Indian. He has intense brown eyes that turn hazel when he's aroused, and a naturally dark complexion. He's just under six feet tall, lean but muscular, and has jet-black hair. My favorite part of the equation is his smile. Bill's whole face lights up when he smiles. I got his voicemail and left a message saying I had to work tonight and asking if he'd be able to sit with Buddy, my dog. Buddy does not like being left home alone. He's a ten-month-old Golden Retriever and Rhodesian Ridgeback mix—ninety-five pounds of muscle and bounce, and the most intelligent dog I've ever met, and I've met a lot of dogs. If Bill couldn't sit with him,

I could ask my neighbor Kirk. Buddy and Kirk's dog D'Artagnon are best buds.

After leaving the message for Bill I looked down at the floor where Buddy was positioned in his usual spot between me and the door. He hadn't stirred since I'd introduced him to Brooke. Apparently he didn't perceive her as a threat. Probably a good sign.

"I need to make some changes to my schedule," I said to the dog. "Then we'll go for a walk."

At the word *walk* Buddy lifted his head and chuffed softly, his eyes bright.

I pulled up the Excel workbook that I use for scheduling bar and restaurant surveys. This is what I do to pay the rent. I eat and drink and watch employees, reporting to the owners of these establishments on service, quality of cuisine and, occasionally, who is stealing them blind. It's a living.

After rescheduling tonight's surveys I called Jessica at the Garden Grill and reserved a table that would allow me and Jim to watch Stanley and Brooke without being obvious about it. Then I asked her about Stanley.

"He's been a regular for years," she said. "Why are you asking?"

"Just between you and me, right?"

"Of course."

"His girlfriend, Brooke, is my client. Stanley recently proposed, and I'm just getting her some background information on him. She tells me he always sits at my favorite table."

"That's right, and he always has the same server. Poor Jaime hasn't had a Friday night off in over a year."

"What happens if Jaime isn't available?"

"The last time that happened I volunteered to serve Stanley myself, and he got up and left."

"Yikes."

"Yeah."

CHAPTER 3

STANLEY GODARD WAS ON EDGE. Normally he felt pretty much in control of what occurred in his world, but lately things seemed to be veering out of balance, and balance was extremely important to Stanley. For one thing, Brooke had yet to accept his proposal. This made him feel vulnerable, and vulnerability made him feel out of control.

In order to compensate for the one thing he had absolutely no influence over, Brooke's decision, he found himself trying desperately to organize everything else. He had a new client who had asked him to perform an audit, and much to Stanley's dismay, when he started work on the job he found the company was missing some essential records. He had spoken with the CFO who had requested the audit, but the documents still hadn't been delivered to him, leaving him with a low key sense of anxiety.

Stanley suspected the CFO might be trying to put one over on him. All he was asking for were invoice and check copies for some large payments the company had made to a vendor. How could someone misplace invoice and check copies? The sum of the payments was over three hundred thousand dollars. Surely they didn't expect him to sign off on the audit without evidence that the money had actually been paid to a legitimate vendor.

As a last ditch effort Stanley went online, searching for the company to whom the payments had been made. If he could contact their accounts receivable manager, they should be able to supply him with the invoice copies. But Stanley couldn't find the vendor online. He put in a call to his client's accounts payable department and asked the clerk who answered for the vendor's phone number. When the AP clerk said she'd have to get back to him, Stanley's anxiety level ratcheted up a notch.

He wasn't a patient man, but he forced himself to wait twenty-four hours before calling the AP clerk back. This time he got her voicemail and the outgoing message said that she was on an indefinite leave of absence. Stanley was shaking when he replaced the receiver in its cradle.

Chapter 4

Bill called me back at 5:00, saying he could be at the marina by 6:30, and would be happy to sit with Buddy tonight. Relieved, I showered, primped, and slipped into a flirty turquoise strapless dress I'd found on sale at Macy's. Bill and I had spent some time sailing last weekend, and I was anxious to show off my tan.

I paired the dress with taupe ankle strap sandals, and added an American Indian necklace of silver beads and turquoise stones that Bill had given to me on Valentine's Day. I'd actually purchased the dress because it set off the necklace so perfectly. If I didn't stop buying new clothes pretty soon I'd have to do a purge of my hanging locker and see what could be stowed in the built-in bunk drawers. My reflection seemed pleased with the results and when Bill showed up at 6:25 he was equally pleased and, shortly thereafter, I found myself in the shower again.

I arrived at the Garden Grill at 7:25 and spent a few minutes catching up with Jessica, who was acting as hostess tonight. Jessica James is five-foot-five and a hundred and twenty pounds of dynamite. She has long, slightly wavy brown hair, and an exquisite sense of fashion. Tonight she was wearing a cobalt blue and white chiffon dress that was almost translucent with a pair of blue Badgley Mischka pumps. The colors in the dress perfectly set off her dark hair and eyes.

We talked until the next patron arrived and I was escorted to my table. Jim came in moments later. I waved to get his attention. After joining me, he gave me a quick once over, taking in the strapless dress, then pecked me on the cheek and said, "You look great, Nikki."

"Thank you, Jim. And thank you for working with me on this one."

I'd printed out my notes from the interview with Brooke and made a copy of Stanley's photo. I handed the pages to Jim and watched silently as he read them. Jim is just over six feet tall, with red hair and fair skin. He's solidly built, intensely loyal, and has a wry sense of humor.

When he'd finished reading he looked up and grinned. "This might be interesting."

I knew he was talking about Brooke's history with men. I'd been thinking about that too. "You know what strikes me?" I said. "I understand Brooke made a decision to change the kind of guys she was seeing, but you can't choose who you're attracted to. There must be something a little bit bad about Stanley. Something that drew her to him. They've been dating for eleven months. You don't spend that much time with someone if you're not attracted to them."

"Good point. Maybe he's a wolf in sheep's clothing."

Jessica came over to take our drink orders and I introduced her to Jim. She gave him a dazzling smile and shook his hand firmly, then told us about the specials.

Our drinks had been served and our waiter, Jaime, was taking our dinner orders when Brooke and Stanley were escorted past our table. If Brooke noticed me, she didn't let on. Jaime saw them go by and rolled his eyes, but said nothing. He collected our menus and hurried off to the kitchen.

I nudged Jim and inclined my head toward

the glass-walled room where the couple was being seated. He smiled appreciatively as he looked Brooke over. Fortunately, she was going to be sitting with her back to us. Stanley was on the other side of the table, facing her, so we'd be able to observe his behavior throughout the evening.

Jaime returned from the kitchen and presented menus to Brooke and Stanley. I wondered if Brooke always ordered the same beverage and entrée to appease Stanley and his need for routine. That would be a shame. Most of the items on the Garden Grill's menu are Jessica's own original recipes, and each is a culinary masterpiece. I've often wondered how she keeps her figure. Just inhaling the tantalizing aromas in the restaurant makes my waistline expand. Maybe it's metabolic. Jessica is so full of energy that she reminds me of a perpetual motion machine. She also has an impressive IQ, matched only by her creative brilliance in the kitchen.

Tonight I was starting with the Devils on Horseback appetizer (bacon-wrapped prunes stuffed with crunchy almond chutney), and had ordered the Prawns 'Dublin Lawyer' entrée, which is sautéed in Irish whiskey and cream. Just thinking about it made me salivate. Jim had requested the Grilled

Salmon Fillet with White Wine and Shallots. There was a basket of cheese scones on the table, which is what the Garden Grill offers in place of a traditional basket of French bread. I was doing my best to ignore these succulent offerings, since I know they're made with loads of butter and extra sharp cheddar, but the flaky delicacies were calling out to me. It was only a matter of time.

Jaime returned from the bar with a bottle of wine which he uncorked at Stanley and Brooke's table. He poured a small amount into Stanley's glass, and Stanley inhaled the bouquet, took a sip, and savored for a moment before nodding. Jaime poured half a glass for Brooke and did the same for Stanley, then set the bottle on the table after carefully wiping the neck with a white dishtowel he carried over his arm. He silently accepted their orders, collected the menus, and departed, his eyes heavenward.

Jaime Antonio Garcia is a gem. He's been with Jessica since she opened the restaurant and I've been served by him countless times, so I knew him to be exceptionally patient. If Stanley got on his nerves it was not without cause.

The evening was relatively uneventful until the dishes had been cleared from

Brooke and Stanley's table, and Jaime had taken the couple's dessert order. As he moved away from their table I saw Stanley reach into his pocket and take out a ring box. He unceremoniously popped it open and set it in front of Brooke, who sat stone-still for a few moments, then apparently said something that was not the response Stanley had been hoping for. He reached forward, snapped the ring box shut, and slipped it back into his pocket.

Jaime returned at that moment with two dishes of peach cobbler. As he set them on the table Stanley's face convulsed in some kind of a spasm, like a twitch fueled by extra voltage. He put his fingertips to his right temple in an effort to quiet the errant musculature. Before Jaime could escape, Stanley held out a credit card. Apparently he'd lost his appetite.

Their desserts remained untouched and neither of them said a word as they waited for Jaime to return with the check. Stanley signed the credit card slip, pocketed his card and the receipt, and stood. Brooke remained seated and Stanley walked behind her chair and pulled it out as she slowly rose. Then he followed her out of the restaurant, his face clenched in a grimace.

"Wow," Jim said, when they were out of earshot. "He doesn't take rejection well."

"I don't think she even rejected him. I think she just asked for more time."

I left enough cash on the table to cover the check and Jaime's tip, and we hustled outside in time to see Stanley and Brooke pulling away in a Volvo station wagon. I jumped into my little BMW 2002 and gave chase. After a couple of blocks I spotted Jim's Bimmer behind me. Jim leases several anonymous looking vehicles, which he and his agents use for surveillance, but tonight he was driving his personal car, a new Mediterranean Blue BMW 3 Series sedan.

We caravanned along behind Stanley's Volvo to highway 101 north, then Jim dropped back while I stayed closer to the subject vehicle. I kept my eyes peeled for anyone else who might be tailing the couple, even though it didn't make sense for Stanley to have Brooke followed when she was with him. The Volvo stayed just below the speed limit, making it easy to shadow.

I called Jim on my cell when Stanley pulled into the slow lane. "He's taking the Holly Street exit," I said. "Brooke lives in a Redwood Shores condo complex, so he's probably taking her home. You have the address on the report I gave you. I'm going to pull over and let you take the lead so you can see where they park. You stay with Brooke and I'll follow Stanley when he leaves."

I pulled over on Redwood Shores Parkway and waited until Jim drove past, then followed at a distance. When I reached the condo complex I hit redial and Jim picked up.

"Where are they?" I asked.

"Volvo's parked in the lot nearest the street. They're both out of the car, heading toward the apartments."

I cruised around the lot until I spotted Jim's BMW, then killed my lights and pulled into a vacant parking space. I dug in my purse for my copy of the report I'd given to Jim and looked up Stanley's home address. He lived off Ralston Avenue in Belmont, not far from his office in downtown San Carlos. I looked around the well-lit parking lot and located Stanley's Volvo.

Only a few minutes passed before Stanley reappeared and unlocked his car. I waited until he'd pulled onto the Parkway, then started up the Bimmer and followed.

Jim and I were still connected, so I told him I was going to call Brooke to make sure she was okay and to let her know that he would be outside until midnight. We disconnected and I turned on my dome light long enough to read her home number at the top of the report. I shut off the light and dialed by touch. Brooke didn't answer and my heart started racing, imagining what Stanley might have done to her. When her answering machine picked up I started to leave a message, but was interrupted as soon as I'd announced who I was.

"Nicoli, thank goodness it's you. I was afraid it was Stanley."

"Are you okay?" I asked.

"I'm fine. Just a little shaken up. Did you see what happened after dinner?"

"I saw the ring box, if that's what you mean."

"Can you *believe* that? When he originally proposed I told him I needed time to think about it. It's only been a week! I was so shocked tonight, I didn't know what to say. Finally I just told him I wasn't ready. What else could I do? I care about Stanley, but lately I feel like I don't really know him."

"So what happened after you left the restaurant? Did he say anything?"

"Not a word. He looked like he was going to explode, though. I'm worried about him."

"Did he walk you to your door when he brought you home?"

"Yes, but he didn't come in. He just said, 'Goodnight, Brooke,' and walked away."

"Okay. I guess that's good. My associate Jim Sutherland is parked outside, keeping an eye on you."

I gave her Jim's cell number and told her to call him if anything out of the ordinary happened. I didn't know what that might be, but I thought it would make her feel more secure, knowing someone was nearby.

"He'll be there until midnight and he has your number so he can call you if he sees anything suspicious. Is your door locked?"

"Locked and deadbolted."

"Good. I'm following Stanley. I'll talk to you tomorrow."

"Okay. Thank you, Nicoli."

"Call me Nikki."

We disconnected and I rang Jim back to let him know that Brooke was fine and that she had his number. He hadn't seen anyone lurking around the complex, but that didn't mean they weren't there. If he didn't spot a tail after a couple of nights, I was thinking we could have Brooke take a late night drive somewhere isolated, where it would be obvious if she was being followed.

Stanley drove to his home in Belmont, locked his car in the garage, and entered the house through the front door. Apparently the house didn't have a connecting door to the garage. Not so unusual in California where the temperature rarely drops below thirty degrees. I parked down the street and watched as Stanley went from room to room turning on lights. It appeared he was turning on every light in the house. I wondered if that was part of his affliction. I'd done some reading about people with OCD and the importance of their rituals. Some of them apparently fear something horrible will occur if they deviate even slightly from their established routine. I'd also watched Jack Nicholson in *As Good As It Gets*, washing his hands dozens of times a day, each time with a fresh bar of soap. What a way to live.

I remained parked on Stanley's street until a few minutes after midnight and all the lights were still on. I wondered if he slept with the lights on. I couldn't fault him for that. I'm not a big fan of the dark, myself. My cell phone chirped and I picked it up, knowing it would be Jim.

"Everything's quiet here," he said. "I'm heading home."

"Okay. Thank you, Jim."

I decided I might as well get some sleep too, since I needed to be back here first thing in the morning. I started my car and pulled away from the curb. As I passed Stanley Godard's house I thought I detected the slight movement of a curtain. Could he have been watching me all this time? The thought sent a chill down my spine. It's one thing for me to watch other people. I do this for a living. But for someone to watch me watching them totally creeped me out. I reached into my purse and found the American Spirit Organic cigarettes I'd been trying to quit smoking, and lit one on my way to El Camino Real.

Chapter 5

On Saturday morning, after my workout at the gym and a quick breakfast, Bill drove me to the local Alamo Rent A Car. I wasn't sure Stanley had been watching me the night before, but I drive a 1972 BMW model 2002 in British racing green. It's an unusual looking car, and I didn't want to risk being recognized.

Bill dropped me off outside the car rental office and asked when I'd be back.

"I'll be doing surveillance all day, and I have to do surveys on two restaurants and a bar tonight. I thought I'd ask Elizabeth to come along, that is, if you can sit with Buddy again. You know how he hates to be left alone."

Elizabeth Gaultier is my best female friend, and a fellow marina dweller.

"No need for the extra guilt. I'll be happy to stay onboard with the boy."

"Thank you!" I kissed Bill and jumped out of his Mustang, speed dialing Elizabeth on my cell as I strode toward the car rental office. She picked up on the first ring.

"Hi, honey. What are you up to?"

"A full day of surveillance, then two restaurants and one bar survey tonight. I need a beard and some girl time. Are you free?"

"I'm at Jack's right now, but I'll be home by five. What time are you picking me up?"

"Seven-thirtyish?"

"Perfect. I'll have time to primp. Are we going anyplace special?"

"Bos in San Francisco, Benedetto in Belmont, and Caliente Bistro in Palo Alto."

"Sounds fattening. You know I'm dieting so I can fit into my wedding dress."

"Your wedding isn't for sixteen months."

"Fifteen and a half months, and I don't want to leave anything until the last minute."

"You know Jack would love you even if you gained fifty pounds, right?"

Jack "The Cat" McGuire was a recently retired cat burglar to whom I'd introduced Elizabeth last August while I was working on a case for him. The rest, as they say, is history. The attraction between my best friend and my client was immediate, and as the two redheads got to know each other it had quickly developed into one of those storybook romances. He'd met her in August and proposed in October. I wasn't the least bit jealous that my friend had found true love. I was content in my relationship with Bill, and a lifetime commitment was the last thing on my mind.

"Of course I know that," Elizabeth said, interrupting my thoughts. "But I want to look perfect for my wedding anyway. Besides, who knows how long I'll have my figure."

I'd just entered the Alamo office, but stopped mid-stride. "What do you mean? You're not pregnant are you?"

"Of course not. Jeez, Nikki, take a breath. I'm just planning for the future. My mom said she never got her figure back after I was born."

"Your mom's a perfect size two, Elizabeth."

Of course I'd only seen photos. Elizabeth's mother still lived in New Orleans, where Elizabeth had grown up, and in the years we'd known each other had never paid her only child a visit. From what I understand about their relationship, Elizabeth is fine with that.

"That's true. How should I dress tonight?"

"I'm wearing jeans and a halter top."

"Gotcha. Sexy casual. I'll see you at seven-thirty."

We ended the call, and I felt the familiar ache in my chest at the thought of my best friend moving out of the marina to Jack's estate in Hillsborough. Even though Hillsborough is only a fifteen minute drive from Redwood City, I knew I'd miss Elizabeth more than I was willing to admit to her. I wouldn't spoil her happiness for anything.

By 8:45 I was seated in a beige Toyota Corolla at the corner of Stanley's street, hoping he was still at home. My hair was pulled up in a ponytail and I was wearing dark glasses. He couldn't have gotten a good look at me last night in the dark, but there was no sense taking chances.

At 8:47 Stanley exited the front door carrying a briefcase. I scrunched down in my seat. He locked the door behind him and opened the garage. He backed the Volvo into the driveway, then got out of the car and closed and locked the garage door. In the daylight I was better able to appraise the house. It looked to me like it had been built in the last ten years. I couldn't help wondering why Stanley didn't have an automatic garage door. Maybe it was a safety issue, or the fear that if the power went out he wouldn't be able to get the door open.

When he got to the corner I started my engine and followed. We took Ralston Avenue to El Camino Real and went south toward San Carlos. I assumed he was headed for his office, and I was right. He made a right turn on San Carlos Avenue and then a left on Laurel Street, drove five blocks, and parked in a small lot in front of an unpretentious single-story office building. The signage read *Stanley A. Godard, CPA.*

I parked on the street, far enough away to be inconspicuous, but close enough to see his front door. Stanley got out of the Volvo with his briefcase, and went inside. He turned on the office lights, then turned them off, then on, then off again. He did this seven times. I didn't remember him flipping the lights on and off when he got home last night. I know OCD sufferers have strict rituals and routines they follow. Maybe these change depending on the location. My heart went out to Stanley, trying to live a normal life with this emotionally crippling affliction.

I was contemplating what it must be like to live with compulsions you had no control over, and considering my own desire for cigarettes, when a brand new silver Mercedes sedan pulled into Stanley's parking lot. I took out my mini binoculars and tried to get a look at the license plate, but the driver parked the car with its side to me. A tall, well-built man in his forties, dressed in business casual, got out of the car carrying a small suitcase. Financial records? He beeped the car locked and entered the office.

I noted the time and a description of the man and his car, and settled in for what promised to be a long day of watching Stanley's clients come and go. Maybe he was open on Saturdays so they could visit his office without missing work.

It was already warm outside so I started the engine, turned on the air conditioning, and rolled up the windows.

After about five minutes I heard a faint popping sound. I supposed it could have been a car backfire, but the automatic clench in my gut told me otherwise. I knew that sound. I looked around, but there were no cars driving by at the moment. I was scanning the neighborhood for any signs of a threat when Stanley's client burst out of the office, unlocking the Benz with his remote as he ran. I grabbed the binoculars, hoping to get the plate number as he exited the lot. As I raised them to my eyes I caught a glimpse of his face. It was a mask of terror. An instant later he was in his car. I held the binoculars with one hand and reached for my notepad with the other, but as the Mercedes turned to pull out of the lot an old rusted-out orange VW van slowly rolled by, sputtering and coughing, and blocked my view of the Benz, which shot off in the other direction.

I kept the binoculars up until the van had passed, hoping the Benz would still be close enough for me to get at least a partial plate number, but I was out of luck. I cursed under my breath, wondering why Stanley's client was in such a hurry, and concerned about what might have caused that popping sound. I quickly checked my watch and logged the time on my notepad, then turned my attention back to Stanley's office.

The look on the guy's face as he'd run outside was really bugging me. I thought about going inside to make sure everything was okay, but the timing of the events told me to be cautious. Besides, if I went inside Stanley would know what I looked like and I'd have to get Jim to follow him in the future.

The next four minutes passed like

molasses and then *KABOOM!* The small building exploded with a deafening roar and enough force to blow the roof off, sending a shock wave through the Corolla. Car alarms sounded throughout the neighborhood as the roof plummeted back down and crashed on top of Stanley's Volvo. I scrambled for my cell phone and dialed 911 as I lunged out of the car and ran across the street. The dispatcher answered and I quickly shouted the address, telling her there had been someone inside the building when it blew up. She took my name and cell number and instructed me not to approach the building.

I disconnected and stood on the sidewalk looking at the destruction and breathing in the acrid, smoke-filled air. All the windows had blown out and there was glass, smoldering wood, and shingles strewn across the parking lot. Black smoke billowed thickly into the sky. There was no wind so the adjacent buildings would probably be spared. Still, I felt obligated to run around knocking on doors to make sure everyone near Stanley's office was aware of the fire. Even though they couldn't have missed the explosion, I wanted them to know it had already been called in.

The San Carlos Fire Department was on

Elm Street, maybe six blocks from Stanley's office. I hoped they had an engine available and were on their way.

I called Bill. I was shaking from the adrenaline rush and needed to hear the voice of someone who loved me. After telling Bill what had happened and assuring him that I was okay and there was no reason for him to come to my rescue, I called Jim.

"I think our job has been cancelled," I said. "The client's boyfriend just got blown up."

CHAPTER 6

"TELL ME EVERYTHING," JIM SAID calmly.

"I followed Stanley to his office this morning. He met with a client at nine-oh-five, then the client left and the office exploded."

I heard sirens approaching and covered my ear so I could hear Jim.

"Tell me about the client," he said.

"He was driving a new silver Mercedes sedan. Nice looking guy, tall, in his forties, carrying a small suitcase."

"I assume he left before the explosion. Did he have the suitcase when he came outside?"

I thought back. "No, he didn't. You think there was a bomb in the suitcase?"

"Maybe. Did you get his plate number?"

"No."

"Did anything else happen before the explosion?"

"I heard a popping sound. I had the air conditioning on and the windows rolled up, so it wasn't clear. Might have been a car backfiring, but my gut reacted like it was a gunshot."

The police, fire department, and EMTs had arrived in force and the street was now crowded with onlookers, as well as smoke and debris. There was a lot of commotion, and I needed to talk to the cops.

"I'll have to call you back, Jim," I said, and disconnected.

My eyes were burning and my nose was running from the smoke as I approached a uniformed officer who was attempting to control the crowd and told him my name. "I'm the one who called this in," I said.

He looked me over, then pulled his radio off his belt. "It's Murphy, sir," he said into the microphone clipped to his collar. "The woman who called dispatch is out here. Yes sir." He clipped the radio back onto his belt and said, "Sergeant Aimes wants you to wait here. He needs to ask you some questions."

"Sure," I said. "Any chance the guy in the office survived?" I knew the answer, but

I also knew that I was going to have to tell Brooke that Stanley was dead, and I wanted corroboration before I made that phone call.

The cop turned his head and looked at the smoldering remains of the building. "No way," he said.

I pointed at the rented Corolla and said, "I'll be waiting in my car. I need to make a couple of phone calls." His expression told me he didn't like that idea, so I said, "I promise I'm not going to leave," and turned away before he could respond.

The fire department had cordoned off the street around Stanley's office building, but luckily I'd parked far enough away that I'd be able to get out when the time came. I closed myself up in the car and dug out my cigarettes, grateful that I'd requested a rental in which I could smoke. I lit one and hit redial on the cell. Jim answered instantly.

"I only have a minute," I said, "I have to call Brooke and the cops want to talk to me. I need to reach her before they do."

"Because..."

"Because I don't want some stranger telling her that Stanley is dead."

"Okay. Call me back after you're done there."

We disconnected and I found Brooke's

number on my smartphone. I pressed send, hoping she was home. I glanced out the window as the phone rang. The TV crews were arriving, and I was relieved to be in the car. I didn't need my face on the six o'clock news again. I'd just gotten back some of the clients I lost after the last time my photo was publicized. Brooke's answering machine picked up. *Please don't let her be watching television*, I silently prayed.

"Brooke, it's Nikki. If you're there…"

"Nicoli?"

"Yes. Thank God you're home."

"What's wrong?"

"Something terrible has happened, Brooke. Are you sitting down?"

"You're scaring me."

"Sorry. Just sit, okay?"

"All right, I'm sitting."

"Brooke, I'm so sorry, but Stanley's office just blew up, and he was inside. He's dead."

My announcement was met with silence. I waited. Finally she said, "That's not funny."

"I'm not joking. I'm in San Carlos across the street from his office. I saw it happen."

"That's impossible. I just talked to him."

"When?"

"He called me this morning to apologize for his behavior last night. Said he was sorry for rushing me, and that he was willing to wait as long as it took for me to make a decision."

"What time did he call?"

"I don't know, around eighth-thirty I guess. I was having breakfast."

"The explosion was a little after nine." I looked out the car window at the news vans crowding the street. "Turn on channel four."

I spotted an older cop approaching my car. "I've got to go, Brooke. I have to give a statement to the police, and I need your permission to tell them why I'm here."

"Of course," she whispered. I could hear TV sounds on the other end of the phone. She was starting to believe me.

"I'm sorry," I repeated. "I'll call you back in a little while."

I slipped the phone into my pocket, snagged my notebook, and got out of the car. Sergeant Aimes was a tall, gray-haired man, solidly built, maybe fifty. He looked like he worked out, but his once handsome face had been hardened by years of dealing with situations most people couldn't imagine. I wondered if Bill would eventually become hard around the edges too.

After we'd introduced ourselves, he

said, "Are you the one who called this in to dispatch?"

"Yes. I was watching the office for a client. I'm a PI." I gave him my business card and told him Brooke's name and phone number. He wrote them down.

"Why?" he asked.

"Excuse me?"

"Why did Ms. Evans want you to watch the office?"

"The tenant, Stanley Godard, had proposed to her, and she wanted me to get some background info before accepting. I assume you'll be contacting her. She can give you the details."

He didn't like my answer, but apparently decided to accept it for the moment.

"What time did you arrive here this morning?"

I consulted my notebook. "Eight fifty-five."

"And then what happened?"

I told him about Stanley's client in the Benz, about the popping sound I'd heard, the noisy VW van, and, finally, the explosion.

"I don't suppose you got the plate number of the Mercedes," he said.

"The van blocked my view. The client had a small suitcase with him when he went inside," I said, "but not when he came back out."

He looked at me. "You think there might have been a bomb in the suitcase?"

"It's possible. At the time I thought it might be financial records."

"Huh."

He wrote my home and cell phone numbers on the business card I'd given him and thanked me for my time. I got back in the Corolla. There was no point in hanging out here any longer. I started the engine, dialed Brooke's number, and put the phone on speaker mode as I pulled away from the curb and made a U-turn, navigating around double parked news vans.

This time Brooke picked up after one ring.

"How are you doing?" I asked.

"I can't believe it's true," she said, sounding dazed. "I turned on the TV and I saw the office, or what's left of it. Are you sure he was in there?"

"Pretty sure. I saw him go in the front door and I didn't see him come out again. Did the office have a back door?"

"Yes."

"Well, then there's a remote possibility

he went out the back before the building blew up."

"I guess a remote chance is better than none," she said wistfully. "What should I do?"

"The police will be in touch with you. When you talk to them, ask if they recovered a body from the scene. They'll want to know why you hired me. Tell them as much as you're comfortable with."

"What did you tell them?"

"I said you wanted some background information on Stanley before you accepted his proposal."

"Thank you, Nicoli."

"Please, call me Nikki. Let me know what the police tell you about Stanley's body." I cringed at the way that sounded. "Sorry, Brooke."

We disconnected and I called Jim on my way to the marina. He asked me to go over the sequence of events again.

"I followed Stanley from his house to his office. Watched him turn the lights on and off seven times. The guy in the Mercedes arrived with his suitcase and went inside. I heard the popping sound. The client ran out of the office and got in his car. He looked totally freaked. As he was driving away I tried to get his plate number, but an old VW rattle-trap van drove by and blocked my view. Four minutes later the office blew up. I called nine-one-one and reported the explosion. Then the police, EMTs, and fire department arrived, followed by the press."

"How long before the client ran out did you hear the popping sound?"

"Only a few seconds."

"So if it was a gunshot, maybe the client shot Stanley, or he was in the office when someone else did."

"According to Brooke, there was a back door. I could only see the front door from where I was parked."

"Maybe the killer was inside waiting for Stanley, but then the client came in."

"If that's the case, why wouldn't he wait until the client was gone?"

"I don't know. Bomb was on a timer?"

We tossed ideas back and forth until I pulled into the marina parking lot. I told Jim I'd let him know if I heard anything else. Maybe Bill could use his connections to get the autopsy results, providing Stanley's body was in the building when it blew. As much as I wanted to believe he might have escaped the blast, I thought it extremely unlikely.

I walked down to the boat rather than

going to my office. I wanted some time with Buddy and Bill before I sat down at the computer to document the morning from hell.

The marina where I live and work houses five gates, or docks, and about five hundred yachts, half of which are owned by individuals and families who live aboard as I do. The office complex that surrounds the marina is comprised of five two-story, wooden structures which are painted light gray with white trim. The first floor corner offices that face the water, like mine, have almost floor to ceiling windows that slide open. The grounds are lush and well maintained. Just across the street is the Bair Island Wildlife Refuge, which is an excellent place to wander around with your dog.

As I walked down the companionway to the docks I inhaled the scent of the bay combined with the odors of sawdust and varnish from the many boat owners who choose to spend their weekends working on maintenance projects.

I was halfway down the dock when Bill and Buddy came out to meet me.

"Buddy saw you come in the gate," Bill said, by way of explanation.

"What a smart boy."

I gave each of them a hug and felt my pulse slow to normal again.

We all sat in the main salon watching the local news report. Someone's remains were being wheeled out of Stanley's office in a black body bag, and loaded into the coroner's van.

I turned to Bill. "You know anyone with the SCPD?"

"A few people. Who caught the case?"

"I spoke with Sergeant Aimes."

"He's good, but he's not a detective. He'll pass it off to either Abrahams or Faulkner."

"I need to know if Stanley was shot before he got blown up."

I told him about the sound I'd heard before the client ran out of the office.

"I'll see what I can find out."

"Thanks."

After more human and canine hugs, I shuffled up to my office.

CHAPTER 7

I TRIED TO APPRECIATE THE BEAUTIFUL day as I walked along the dock, but I just couldn't get the experience of the explosion out of my head. My clothes and hair reeked of the acrid smoke. I asked myself who would want to kill a CPA. Had Stanley uncovered something illegal that one of his clients wanted to keep hidden? I thought about the guy who had visited Stanley this morning and the look of panic on his face when he ran out of the office. He hadn't looked like a killer to me, but I'd only seen him from a distance. Besides, maybe it was his first time. That could account for the horror. I remembered when I'd had to kill someone, and the shock that swallowed me up afterwards. But *I* hadn't planned a murder. I had acted in self-defense.

I unlocked the office and absently pressed the play button to access my messages. Brooke's voice filled the room.

"Hi, Nikki. The police just left. They said they found a body in the rubble and they think it was Stanley. They're probably right. Who else could it be?" Her voice cracked slightly. "They asked me if I knew who his dentist was. I guess the body was badly burned," she choked on the words. "Anyway, I told them I hired you because Stanley's behavior had changed since he proposed. They wanted details. I felt like I was betraying Stanley, but I told them everything. The detective wrote it all down and said he'd contact me when they have a positive ID. Could you call me back when you get this message?" She left her home number.

I took a deep breath and dialed.

"Thanks for calling me back," she said. "I want you to find out who did this to Stanley."

My stomach clenched. I'd handled homicide investigations before and while I enjoy a challenge I do not enjoy putting myself in the line of fire. But how could I turn her down?

"Who's the detective in charge of the case?" I asked.

"Hang on, he gave me his card." She set the phone down and moments later came back on the line. "Detective Faulkner."

"Did he seem incompetent to you?"

"No. Quite the opposite. He seemed very bright and kind of intense."

"So why do you need me?"

"Well, I know you, sort of, and I know you'll tell me anything you find out. Plus this isn't Faulkner's only case."

"I have other clients, Brooke."

"Please, Nikki. I need a friend right now."

She had me cornered. "Okay, I'll look into it," I sighed. "Next time you talk to Faulkner tell him I'm conducting an independent investigation and you'd appreciate it if he would speak with me."

"I can do that."

"And call me as soon as they ID the body."

"Okay. Thank you."

"Don't thank me yet." That was the voice of my mentor, Sam Pettigrew. Sam was a retired police detective gone private, and the crusty old PI who'd trained me. At some point during the two years I'd spent working with him his voice had gotten stuck in my head and now it pops out during times of stress, whether I like it or not.

I called Bill and told him Detective

Faulkner had caught Stanley's case. He called me back five minutes later and said he'd put in a call to the SCPD and left a message asking Faulkner to get back to him.

After a long soapy shower, during which I shampooed twice, I dressed in stretchy black jeans, a black halter top, and black boots. I gelled and scrunched my curls and applied mascara and lip gloss. I moved my Ruger from the fanny pack holster to my black pistol purse, which I draped over my shoulder.

When I stepped into the galley where Bill was working on his laptop, his look of appreciation made all the effort worthwhile.

"Are you sure you have to work tonight?" he asked, waggling his eyebrows.

"Sorry, but yes. Brooke's case will occupy my days, and my regular clients deserve some attention too."

I gave him a kiss, scooped some kibble into Buddy's dish, and grabbed a light jacket.

Elizabeth's trawler door was open when I approached her dock steps, and I could hear the theme song for Entertainment Tonight coming from the TV mounted in her galley. For a woman with an IQ in the 'extremely gifted' range, Elizabeth is inexplicably drawn to movie and TV star gossip.

I knocked on the open door, and she popped in from the stateroom. Dressed in a lime green mini dress, my diminutive thirty-four-year-old friend looked like a feisty high school cheerleader. Elizabeth has strawberry blond hair, hazel eyes, dimples, freckles, and weighs about a hundred pounds. Since she's just over five feet tall, the weight is perfect for her.

"Hi, honey. You look great!"

"So do you! Ready to go?"

"Just let me set up the DVR. I don't want to miss what's happening with Ryan Gosling. Did you know he and Eva Mendes have a little girl?"

"Um… no?"

I waited patiently while she programmed her DVR, then locked up the trawler. As we walked up the companionway to shore she chattered on about what was happening with her favorite stars. I listened, sort of, and unlocked my BMW. During a lull in the conversation, or rather monologue, I jumped in.

"I have a new case that's kind of bugging me," I said.

"Ooh. Tell me everything."

"Yesterday I met with a woman who was concerned that her boyfriend was having her followed. She said that after dating for eleven months he'd proposed, and when she asked for some time to think about it he went a little OCD. He started fussing about how clean her condo was, or wasn't, and how much she weighed, and he'd get upset if she was even a minute late for anything. Anyway, she asked me to keep an eye on him, and this morning he got blown up."

"*What?* Holy *shit*! Back up a minute. What did this guy do for a living?"

"Well that's the thing. He was a CPA. Who would want to kill an accountant?"

"Do you think he was into something illegal, or was maybe blackmailing a client who was into something illegal?"

"Anything is possible. Brooke, that's my client, wants me to investigate the murder."

"Oh no. No, no, no. Not again. Nikki, every time you get involved in a murder investigation someone tries to kill you. It's enough already."

"Nina Jezek didn't try to kill me."

"No, she just stun gunned you and left you on the ground, then slashed Lily's tire. Why can't you be happy with restaurant and bar surveillance?"

"Okay, what's wrong? You're always the first one onboard when I have a dangerous case and need help."

"There's nothing wrong. I just don't want anything to happen to you. *Especially* now."

"Why especially now?"

My question was met with silence.

"Elizabeth… why especially now?"

She brushed a tear from her cheek and turned to face me. "I need you, Nikki. I didn't realize how much until I started planning the wedding and realized that when I move to Hillsborough we won't be neighbors anymore." She sniffled and dug in her purse for a tissue. "It's over a year away, and I already miss you." She quietly blew her nose. "And I want you to be my kids' godmother. So you need to be more *careful*." This last sentence was said with a stomp of her size four platform heel on the floorboard of my car.

"Okay. Well, for what it's worth I already miss you too. And I have every intention of being around to watch your kids grow up."

By the time we reached San Francisco and Bos, Elizabeth's tears had dried and we'd promised to see each other at least twice a week after the wedding. She planned to keep her trawler docked at the marina, and she and Jack would be spending some weekends onboard. That made me feel a little better about the future. The wedding was planned for a year from next June, so it was still a long way off, but I'd gotten used to having her just one dock away. In spite of the fact that I was happy she and Jack had found each other, the selfish side of me sometimes regretted making that introduction. Sue me. I'm human.

Bos is located on New Montgomery Street, between Mission & Howard, in the SOMA district of San Francisco. I parked in the Priority Parking lot on 2nd Street and we hoofed it the two blocks to the restaurant.

My mouth started watering as soon as we walked in the door. The wonderful aroma of grilled pork and beef permeated the air. The only thing that might keep me from eating my own bodyweight at this amazing restaurant was the huge painting of a somewhat zaftig nude woman that hung on the wall behind the bar. She was a reminder of what could easily happen to my figure if I indulged myself.

We were seated in a window booth. Our waitress approached, dressed simply in jeans, a short sleeve white blouse, and an apron, and asked if we'd like anything to drink. Elizabeth and I both ordered Perrier, since it was going to be a long night of eating and drinking.

Looking over the menu, I was torn between the Grilled Pork Chops and the Mt. Lassen Trout. What I really wanted was the Sausage Plate, but I was afraid the butterball potato would put me in a carb-induced coma. Eventually the trout won out. When the server returned with our water, I placed my order and turned to Elizabeth.

"I'll have the Roasted Beet Salad, please."

"And for an entrée?" the server asked.

"That is my entrée," Elizabeth smiled. "I'm getting married soon, so I'm watching my weight."

The server smiled sweetly, said, "Congratulations," and collected our menus.

"So tell me more about this new case. Where will you begin?"

"The SCPD detective in charge of the case is named Faulkner. Bill knows him, so he left him a message earlier today. Brooke is also going to ask Faulkner if he'll talk to me about the case. I won't know where to begin until I know if it was the explosion that killed Stanley."

"Hold on. Faulkner, as in William Cuthbert Faulkner, the Nobel laureate?"

"Same last name, different guy," I said, and smiled at my well educated friend.

I told her about the sound I'd heard just before the explosion, which might have been a gunshot, and about the VW van that had blocked my view of the Mercedes license plate.

Our dinner was exquisite, the service very good, and the patrons enthusiastic. It would have been a fine survey, but our waitress made a fatal error. I had paid with plastic, and when she returned with the credit card slip for me to sign I saw that she had added an additional ten dollars to the tip I'd written on the tab. Most people wouldn't have noticed the discrepancy, but I'm paid to notice. I collected the receipt and we moved on to Benedetto in Belmont.

Benedetto is a Northern Italian restaurant with an elegant but warm atmosphere. They have a menu to please almost any palate, with a number of entrées that are surprisingly low in both carbs and calories. They're on Ralston Avenue, just a block from Alameda De Las Pulgas. There was no street parking available at this time of night on a Saturday, so I parked across the street in the Carlmont Shopping Center lot.

It was a good thing I'd made a reservation,

because the place was packed. The hostess, a lovely blonde in her mid-thirties, greeted us warmly and escorted us to a booth with a mirrored wall panel, allowing me to watch the servers and customers without being obvious about it. Excellent. She placed menus on the table and asked if we'd like anything from the bar. This time Elizabeth succumbed to her desire for a tall Mudslide, and I ordered a Campari and soda. The hostess made a note, and said our server would be right with us.

We'd barely had time to glance at the menu when our waiter arrived to serve our drinks. He was in his late twenties with a thick head of dark wavy hair, and wore a white shirt with a black tie and black trousers. He actually looked Italian, which was a nice touch. The young man introduced himself as Anthony, visually if not verbally admired Elizabeth's mini dress, and asked if we'd like to hear the specials. Since part of my job is evaluating waitstaff, of course I nodded.

Anthony extolled the virtues of Orecchiette, which is pasta with sausage, fennel, broccoli rabe, red pepper flakes, and pecorino; and then described the Pansotti all Fiorentina, a spinach and ricotta stuffed pasta served on a bed of tomato sauce and sage. The descriptions of these two specials included a lot of dramatic hand gestures. This guy was definitely Italian.

Even though we'd already consumed one meal, I was drooling again. We asked for a few minutes to look over the menu, and Anthony said, "Very good," nodded once to Elizabeth's shapely legs, and departed to check on his other tables. She giggled happily after he'd moved out of earshot.

I was sorely tempted by the pizza and pasta options the menu offered, but decided to stick to my diet and order the Atlantic Salmon entrée. Elizabeth said she was going to have the Bresaola; thinly sliced air-cured beef served with arugula, and low-fat Grana cheese. Apparently she was sticking to her diet as well. When Anthony returned we made our requests, and he winked at Elizabeth while collecting our menus.

"Are you sure you want to tie yourself down?" I asked, tongue in cheek. "Jack's an amazing guy, but there are so many lovely men just clambering for a chance to go out with you."

Elizabeth cheerfully nudged me with her elbow. "I'm done playing the field, Nikki," she said. "This is it for me. Jack is the ONE."

"Well, I'm happy for you. You know that, right?"

"Of course I do, honey. I just wish the same thing would happen for you."

I raised an eyebrow. "What do you mean? I'm crazy about Bill."

"I know you are, and I know you say you love him, but if he was really the ONE you wouldn't be so hesitant to commit."

"That's not true. Bill's great. I just don't want to screw up a perfectly good relationship by promising to love him forever. Been there, done that."

Elizabeth knows my history. I've been married and divorced three times, and each time I watched the relationship crumble rapidly after saying, "I do." I was not going there again.

"Whatever you say. I just want everyone to be as happy as I am."

I said nothing further on the subject, hoping she would let it drop, and she got the hint.

We were in the middle of our entrées when Bill called me on my cell.

"Can you talk?" he asked.

I gave Elizabeth a thumbs-up as I stepped away from the table, and moved quickly into the hallway leading to the restrooms.

"Okay. Go," I said.

"There was enough of Stanley's fingertips left for a positive ID. Faulkner wants to talk to you."

"Of course he does. I'll call him in the morning."

I felt sad for Brooke. I thought about waiting until tomorrow to give her the news. Then I thought about how I would feel if it had been Bill in that explosion, and my eyes heated up.

"Did he say anything about a gunshot wound?" I asked.

"No, but they haven't done the autopsy yet."

We ended the call and I returned to our table.

"What's up honey?" Elizabeth said. "You look like you just got some bad news."

I leaned in close and told her about the prints proving it was Stanley who had died in the explosion.

"That's not exactly a surprise, is it? It *was* his office that blew up, after all."

"I know. But Brooke was hoping there was some mistake, or that Stanley had escaped out the back door before the explosion."

"This isn't your fault, Nikki. Brooke hired you to watch Stanley, not to be his body guard. You need to let it go." She patted my hand, and resumed eating her low calorie dinner. I sighed and sipped my Campari and soda.

The remainder of our time at Benedetto was delicious, if uneventful. The other diners surrounding us all seemed to enjoy their meals, the atmosphere, and each other. Not that I was complaining, much, but I do like to find something wrong every once in a while, just to prove I'm earning my fees.

Around 10:30 we moved on to Palo Alto and the Caliente Bistro. This would be our last stop of the night, and I was only required to survey the bar area. Caliente served fresh oysters on the half shell, and I was planning to have some for dessert. Maybe that would cheer me up.

I found parking in a public lot on Emerson across the street from the restaurant. We locked the car and made our way to the nearest crosswalk. The evening was cooling off, and Elizabeth tucked her arm through mine and leaned against me, probably for warmth.

We entered Caliente and I steered my friend to the lushly appointed bar. Once we had persuaded a single man to move down one stool, we were able to perch together and observe the crowd and the two very busy bartenders, a man and a woman. Both were wearing black jeans and chartreuse short sleeve shirts.

After a few minutes the woman approached us and asked, "What can I get you tonight?"

"Can I get oysters on the half shell at the bar?" I asked.

"Absolutely."

"Excellent. And I'll have an Erdinger Alkoholfrei. In the bottle is fine." As the name implies, Erdinger is a German non-alcoholic beer with a robust, slightly sweet, flavor.

She turned to Elizabeth, who was looking over the bar selection with wide eyes, never having been to Caliente before. "I'll have the Flying Dog Raging Bitch Ale, please," she said with a giggle, "and the Chocolate Budino."

Ah, there was the Elizabeth I knew and loved. The wedding diet be damned. Chocolate Budino was a flourless *chocolate* torte. I'd have to sneak a bite.

On the way home I checked my watch, wondering if it was too late to call Brooke.

It was almost midnight. She might be asleep. Did I really want to wake her up to tell her Stanley was definitely dead?

I turned to Elizabeth. "Do you think I should call Brooke?"

She cut her eyes to me and shrugged. "I don't know, honey. It might be better to call her in the morning. If you tell her now she won't sleep for the rest of the night."

"I doubt she's sleeping anyway."

"But if she is, and you wake her up, she'll never get back to sleep."

"Crap."

"Detective Faulkner may have called her already."

Somehow that made me feel better. I hate giving people bad news and it didn't get much worse than this. I decided to wait and talk to Brooke in the morning.

CHAPTER 8

I DIDN'T SLEEP MUCH SATURDAY NIGHT, and used that as an excuse to skip my Sunday morning workout. After a light breakfast and three cups of caffeine, Bill followed me to the Alamo car rental place so I could return the Toyota.

When we got back to the marina, I unlocked my office and saw the voicemail light was blinking. I powered up the computer, then pressed the play button on the phone's base unit and went into the kitchenette to make coffee. I stepped back out when I heard Brooke's voice. She was crying and it was hard to understand all the words, but I caught enough to know that Faulkner had called her and told her that Stanley's body had been positively identified. She also said something about an attorney and a will between sobs, but I missed most of that.

When the coffee was ready, I poured myself a mug before returning Brooke's call.

The first thing I said was, "I'm so sorry, Brooke." I'd lost count of how many times I'd told her that, but it seemed appropriate under the circumstances.

"Thank you," she said, and sniffled.

"Your message said something about an attorney?"

"That's right. Stanley's attorney called me. Apparently he had a will and he left everything to me. Can you believe it? I'd known him less than a year."

"What about his family?"

"Stanley was estranged from his family. He hadn't spoken with any of them since college."

"Why?" I can't help myself. I'm nosy.

"I don't really know. Something about his childhood, I think."

I pictured a youngster afflicted with OCD trying to fit into a normal family dynamic. Based on what Brooke had just said, I hypothesized that the family environment might have contributed to whatever had caused Stanley's OCD.

"He left me *everything*," Brooke repeated.

"His house, his office. I didn't even know he owned the property the office was on. And he had life insurance."

"Wow."

"And he left me his orchids."

"His what?"

"Stanley bred orchids. It was his passion. He was a member of the American Orchid Society. He'd developed a new hybrid that he was going to show at the Santa Barbara International Orchid Show next weekend. He asked me to go with him." She wept quietly into the phone.

"I had no idea," I said, taken aback by Brooke's disclosure about Stanley's creative side.

She took a deep breath and let it out with a sigh. "He was so excited. His first bud is just opening. I'm supposed to meet Detective Faulkner at Stanley's house this morning. Can you come with me, please?"

"Sure. What time?"

"I have to be there at ten."

I checked my watch. "I'll pick you up at nine-forty-five."

I knew Faulkner wanted to talk to me about what I'd seen yesterday. Maybe this would save me a trip to the San Carlos PD. For some reason I don't enjoy spending time in police stations. It *might* have something to do with being accused of murder last August.

I typed up my dinner and bar surveys from the previous night, grabbed the Ruger from my gun drawer, made sure it was fully loaded, and called Bill on my way to the parking lot.

"I have to go through Stanley's house with Brooke," I said. "We're meeting Faulkner there. Can you stay with Buddy?"

"You work too many weekends."

"I know. I'll try to get back early so we can spend the afternoon together."

I unlocked my car and dug my fanny pack holster out of the glove box. I took the Ruger out of my purse and secured it in the Velcro compartment of the fanny pack, which I strapped around my waist.

I arrived at Brooke's condo complex at 9:40, and realized I didn't know her apartment number. I fished in my purse for the case notes, even though I remembered leaving them in the office. Luckily I had her home number programmed into my smartphone. I selected the number and pressed send.

She answered on the second ring, sounding subdued.

"Brooke, it's Nikki. I'm in the parking lot. What's your apartment number?"

"I'm in two-B. Come in the side entrance and you'll see stairs on your left."

I locked my purse in the trunk of the 2002 and tucked my keys in the pocket of my cargo shorts. Whoever had killed Stanley was still out there, and since I didn't know why he had been killed, I didn't know that they weren't going to be coming after Brooke next. I shifted the fanny pack holster to my left hip and unzipped the compartment, resting my right hand on the butt of the revolver as I walked up the steps to Brooke's condo.

I knocked, and the door immediately opened. Brooke invited me in, said she would be just a minute, and ducked into one of the bedrooms. The apartment was spacious and decorated with what appeared to be genuine antiques.

"Nice furniture," I said, when she came back into the living room.

"Thank you. Most of it belonged to my parents. I still have some of their things in storage. They had wonderful taste."

The room was spotless. I wondered how long after Stanley's death it would be before Brooke felt comfortable allowing some dust to accumulate, treating herself to a Danish on Sunday morning, or skipping a workout, as I had done today.

Brooke hadn't let her grief affect her sense of style. She was dressed in white shorts and a grass-green, silk tank top, with a pair of gold leather Manolo Blahnik sandals on her pedicured feet. She carried a matching gold clutch and withdrew her keys as we stepped outside. She pulled the door closed and used a key to secure the deadbolt.

"I'm probably just being paranoid," she said, apologetically. "But after what happened to Stanley..."

"A little paranoia is a good thing," I said.

Neither of us said much as we drove to Belmont. When I made the turn onto Stanley's street I immediately noticed the piece-of-shit Chevy parked in front of the house. I pulled into the driveway and hopped out of my car, placing myself between Brooke and the man who was getting out of the Chevy. I slipped my hand into my fanny pack and he caught the movement, holding out his hands to show me they were empty.

"Detective Faulkner?" I said.

"Yeah, I'm Faulkner. You must be Hunter. I've heard about you. Saw your picture in the paper once."

He was in his late thirties, almost six feet

tall, with curly, dark brown hair and a neatly trimmed mustache. His face was handsome, but it held no expression, as though he had trained himself not to betray any emotion. His eyes were dark and intelligent. I could see why Brooke had described him as 'kind of intense'. She joined me on the sidewalk and said, "Good morning, Detective."

He nodded at her and said, "Ms. Evans."

"You mind showing me some ID?" I asked.

Brooke apparently recognized this guy as the man who had interviewed her after Stanley's death, so asking for ID felt like overkill, but you really can't be too careful. Faulkner reached into his jacket and took out his badge wallet, flipped it open, and waited patiently while I examined it.

"Okay. Thanks."

We trooped up to the front door and Brooke turned to Faulkner expectantly. "Do you have the key?" she asked.

"No. I assumed you had a key."

"Stanley never gave me one, but he kept a spare in the greenhouse."

Faulkner and I followed her around the side of the house, through a gate, and into the backyard. As I rounded the corner I spotted the greenhouse. It was the size of a small cottage and it was, of course, pristine. Each pane of glass was brilliant and spotless, except for the one just above the doorknob, which had been broken.

"Oh, my *God*," Brooke gasped.

Faulkner stepped in front of her. "Don't touch anything," he said. "Was this door kept locked?"

"Yes, but it has a combination lock. See?" She pointed to a small keypad to the left of the door.

"You know the combination?"

"Yes. It's my birthday."

"Okay. Go ahead and unlock it, but you two need to stay out here while I go inside."

"But the key to the house is in there."

"Where?"

"It's in a secret drawer. Stanley had it installed in one of the tables."

Brooke entered some numbers on the pad and the door clicked. Faulkner dug a pair of latex gloves out of his pocket, slipped them on, and used two fingers to turn the knob. He pulled the door open and stepped over the broken glass.

Brooke and I stood in the doorway watching him move around the tables, all of which were covered with thriving orchids of different sizes and colors.

After a minute Faulkner said, "Okay, you can come inside, but try not to touch anything."

I followed Brooke into the greenhouse. She moved around the table that filled the center aisle. When she reached the end of the table she stopped in her tracks. "Oh, *no*," she moaned.

"What?" I said. "What happened?"

"The orchid," she whispered. "Stanley's hybrid. It's gone."

Chapter 9

"Poor Stanley," Brooke said, fishing for a tissue in her purse. "This would have killed him, I mean, you know, if he wasn't already dead. He's been working on the development of that hybrid for years. He was going to name it after me. He was so excited. You remember I told you the first bud was just opening? Why would anyone steal it?"

I looked around at maybe fifty potted orchid plants. "Are you sure he didn't just move it? Maybe it's one of these." I gestured at the other plants.

"No. He would never have moved it. 'Everything has its place,' he used to say. That orchid sat right here." She pointed to the end of the table. "It was in a special pot that Stanley had made for it. It was yellow enameled clay with stars cut out so the roots could breathe."

Faulkner and I looked around for a yellow enamel pot, but we didn't find one. All the orchids in the room were in unglazed clay pots.

Finally Faulkner said, "This is a crime scene. We need to get out of here and let the technicians come in and do their thing. Where's the house key?"

Brooke reached under the table where the missing orchid had been positioned and fiddled with some kind of lever. A hidden drawer slid out from under the edge of the table. Very cloak and dagger. Inside the drawer were a brass house key and a book that looked like an old fashioned ledger. Brooke handed the key to Faulkner and took the book out of the drawer before closing it.

"What's that?" I asked.

"Stanley's orchid journal. He documented everything."

The three of us stepped carefully out of the greenhouse and Faulkner called someone on his cell as we walked toward the back of the house. He gave Stanley's address and directions, said he'd be waiting, and ended the call.

Faulkner inserted the key in the lock

and held up his gloved hand. "I'd better go in first."

Brooke and I backed away from the door as Faulkner opened it. Reaching under his jacket in a movement I recognized, he withdrew a Glock from his shoulder holster.

"Wait here, please," he said.

Brooke looked alarmed, but said nothing as she hugged Stanley's journal to her chest. I gently nudged her farther away from the open door, thinking that if someone came out in a hurry she might not have the common sense, or the reflexes, to get out of the way.

Faulkner was inside for about five minutes before he returned to the door and said, "You can come in. It's kind of a mess though."

"Uh oh," Brooke murmured, and I knew what she was thinking. Stanley's house would have been immaculate. If there was a mess, someone else had made it.

We entered through the kitchen. It was immediately evident that the house had been searched. Drawers and cabinets had been pulled open and riffled through and canisters had been emptied on the countertop, leaving a mass of flour, sugar, and coffee grounds. Brooke reached out to close one of the drawers and I grabbed her wrist.

"Best not to disturb any fingerprints," I said.

"Oh. Sorry."

We moved through the kitchen into the living room. It was a sweet little house. Even though the couch cushions had been pushed onto the floor and books had been tossed from their shelves, I could still see the order with which Stanley Godard had lived his life.

Faulkner stood in the middle of the room, his eyes on Brooke. She looked stricken as her gaze flicked around the room.

"Can you to tell me if anything is missing?" he asked.

She looked up and met his gaze. "It would be easier to tell if everything wasn't all jumbled up like this."

She shuffled through the living room, taking everything in, then moved across the front hallway to a small office on the other side of the house. Faulkner and I followed. Brooke stopped in the doorway and said, "His computer is gone. Stanley had a Dell laptop." She pointed at the desk.

We spent about fifteen minutes going through each of the rooms in Stanley's house.

Everything had been searched, including the upstairs bedroom and bathroom. The lid had been left off the toilet tank and was leaning up against the wall. I glanced into the tank and noticed that there were no rust stains. Stanley even cleaned the tank behind his toilet. That was a little bit scary.

By 10:30 we were back in the living room. Faulkner asked me to fill him in on everything I had seen the day before. I was just finishing my story when the crime scene van pulled up. It parked on the street in front of Faulkner's unmarked car, blocking enough of the driveway that I wouldn't be able to get the Bimmer out.

"Tell them we're leaving," I said to Faulkner. "They can park in the driveway."

He opened the front door and shouted something to the driver of the van, who pulled forward on the street and waited.

Faulkner turned to Brooke and I saw something in his eyes that hadn't been there before. It almost looked like compassion.

"I'll be in touch," he said.

I ushered Brooke outside and we got in the 2002. I backed onto the street and the van pulled into the driveway.

Brooke sat quietly, clutching Stanley's journal as I drove her back to Redwood

Shores. I found a vacant space in the complex lot and nosed the BMW in, shutting off the engine.

"You want me to come inside with you?" I asked.

"Would you mind? I don't feel like being alone right now."

As we got out of the car I considered how difficult it might have been for a woman who looked like Brooke to find female friends. Jealousy would have driven away any but the most altruistic.

"Is there anyone you can call to come stay with you for a few days?" I asked.

"I have a cousin I'm close to," she said. "But she lives in North Carolina."

"Is that where you grew up?"

"Yes."

That explained the Southern accent.

"Why don't you invite her for a visit? What kind of work does she do?"

"She's a teacher, but she's taking a semester off to recover from a recent divorce. Maybe I will give her a call."

She unlocked the apartment and we went inside.

"You want coffee?" she asked, turning the deadbolt.

"That sounds good." I almost always want coffee.

Brooke busied herself in the kitchen as I walked through each room, checking inside closets, under beds, and behind the shower curtain. No sign of an intruder.

I went into the kitchen and seated myself on an elegant bar stool on one side of the island. Brooke set a porcelain cup and saucer in front of me.

"Do you take cream?"

"Do you have any low fat, lactose free milk?"

She smiled. "I have low fat, but not lactose free."

"That's fine."

Brooke perched on the stool across from me and gazed into her cup.

"Are you okay?" I asked.

"I guess. I was just thinking about the funeral arrangements. I'm meeting with Stanley's attorney tomorrow. I'm sure there are specific instructions in his will about how he wanted it handled. Stanley was particular about everything, but when he looked at me with those puppy dog eyes of his, none of that mattered."

She dissolved into tears.

I looked around and spotted a box of

tissues on the kitchen counter. I hopped off my stool and fetched the box, setting it in front of Brooke and handing her a tissue.

"Thank you."

Brooke needed someone to talk to, so I mentally took myself off the clock and said, "Tell me about your first date."

She blew her nose delicately and smiled. "Stanley was shy. I met with him a couple of times to go over my taxes. He was cute, sweet, and intelligent, but I knew he'd never ask me out, so I said I wanted to buy him lunch, you know, as a thank you. He seemed surprised and kind of flustered. Then I said I'd let him pick the restaurant and he looked so relieved." She laughed quietly and brushed away a tear.

"Where did you go?"

"To the Garden Grill. Stanley insisted on making the reservation himself. He had a favorite waiter, Jaime, and he wanted to make sure he was working and that the table he liked was available."

"What did you talk about?"

"At first he was quiet and it was kind of awkward, so I told him about my childhood in North Carolina, my parents, my job. Finally he started to relax. That's when he told me about his orchids. He was so passionate about them, he was like a different person."

"What else was Stanley passionate about?"

Brooke got up and refilled our cups, considering the question. "Order," she finally said, settling back onto her stool, "and balance. He loved being a CPA because accounting is all about order and balance." Tears filled her eyes and she dabbed at them with a tissue. "Why would anyone want to kill Stanley?"

"I don't know. But I'll do my best to find out."

I sat with Brooke until a little after 1:00, and then said I had to go. I needed time with my dog and Bill, plus I was hungry.

"Promise you'll call your cousin?" I said, as I stepped outside. She nodded. "And bolt this behind me."

I stood outside her door until I heard the deadbolt slide home. As I turned to walk down the stairs I heard Brooke sobbing through the closed door. I sighed, hoping she would call her cousin and that the cousin would drop everything to come and stay with her. She seemed so alone. Maybe that was something she and Stanley had in common.

I drove back to the marina and stopped

in at my office long enough to tally up the hours Jim and I had put in on Brooke's case. The total barely put a dent in her deposit. I wrote out a check for Jim and set it with the outgoing mail, then locked up the office and walked down to the dock.

I stopped along the way, as I always do, to visit with D'Artagnon, a black Lab who is the marina's self-appointed watch dog. D'Artagnon has always been one of my favorite canines, and not just because he saved me from a psycho-killer last July. He was currently sprawled on the bow of his human's Bluewater 42, and wagged his crooked tail in a circle, like a propeller, as I approached. I leaned in for a canine hug, and he rested his forehead against mine as I scratched behind his ears. Dogs are so much easier than people. I sighed and continued down the dock.

As I approached my boat I could hear Bill playing Greensleeves on his acoustic guitar. He's a skilled musician, and the emotions he thinks he's too manly to express are revealed through his music.

I climbed aboard and barely made it inside the pilothouse before Buddy bounded up the companionway, nearly knocking me over.

"Hello, big dog," I said, ruffling his ears.

I heard the music stop and Bill walked into the galley as I backed down the steps.

"How's Brooke doing?" he asked.

"Not so good." I wrapped my arms around him and hung on longer than usual, enjoying the warmth of his body, breathing in the scent of his Gray Flannel cologne, and feeling lucky that I wasn't Brooke Evans.

"I heard from Faulkner again," he said into my hair.

I pulled back and looked up at him. "What did he have to say?"

"He said you nearly drew your gun before he could identify himself this morning."

"I was being cautious."

"He didn't seem to mind. That's not why he called, though. He's had the tech-heads at the SCPD working on the computer that got blown up in Stanley's office. Apparently some of the files on his hard drive were recoverable. Stanley used his Outlook address book and calendar to keep track of his clients. Faulkner wants you to drive around with him tomorrow to see if you can ID the guy in the Mercedes."

"And did it occur to Detective Faulkner to call me directly with this request?"

"I think he was hoping I could convince you to go along."

"And how, exactly, are you planning to do that?"

"I'm going to suggest that this would be an opportunity for you to pick his brain about Stanley's murder."

"Well done, Detective. I'll give him a call."

Chapter 10

DETECTIVE FAULKNER PICKED ME UP at the marina at 8:30 on Monday morning. I was dressed in my traditional spring and summer uniform of Eddie Bauer cargo shorts, a short-sleeved cotton shirt (this one was white), and New Balance Cross Trainers. I was ambivalent about driving around all day in a non-smoker's car, even though I was trying to quit again, but as I settled into the passenger seat I noticed the lingering scent of cigar smoke. I located the ashtray in the console and popped it open. Sure enough, there was a cigar butt crammed into the ashtray.

"You're a smoker?" I asked.

"I am. You?"

"I'm trying to quit. Again."

"Good luck with that."

Our first stop was a family-run drycleaners on Arguello in Redwood City. The owner's name was José Castillo. Didn't sound like the guy I'd seen in Stanley's parking lot, but no stone unturned. We pulled into a small lot to the right of the building. A candy apple red Cadillac was parked against the fence at the back of the lot. Unless I missed my guess the Caddie belonged to Castillo.

We entered through the front door and were immediately struck by a wall of heat. A side door to the lot was open, and two fans set on high were pointed toward the front of the shop, but the temperature still had to be at least a hundred degrees.

After a moment a blond man in his thirties, built like a linebacker, ventured forward.

"Mr. Castillo?" Faulkner asked.

The man nodded once and smiled. It was a very nice smile.

"I'm Detective Faulkner with the San Carlos Police Department." Faulkner flashed his badge. "This is Nicoli Hunter. We're here about Stanley Godard. I assume you've heard about his death."

The smile disappeared.

"Yes," he said.

"I understand you were a client of Mr. Godard's."

Another nod. "He handled our bookkeeping and our taxes."

"When was the last time you saw him?"

"February first," he said without hesitation. "I always brought him our receipts on the first of the month. On Monday, February first, I brought him all of our receipts for January."

I tried not to think about the fire destroying all of Castillo's records. At least it would only be for one month.

"Did anything seem to be bothering him?" Faulkner asked.

"No. He seemed fine to me."

"Did you notice anyone hanging around outside the office when you were there?"

"No. Sorry."

"Okay. Thank you for your time."

When we were back in the car I asked, "Why can't you run a DMV report on each of Stanley's clients? See which one owns a new Benz?"

"We're doing that, but there are too many variables."

"Like what?"

"Well, since the Mercedes was new, it might not be registered yet. Or it could be a company car, not registered to the individual in question."

"How many clients did Stanley have?"

Faulkner handed me a list and I scanned it quickly. There were at least thirty names and addresses, and more than half of them had been highlighted. I looked more closely and saw that the names which had not been highlighted were women.

"Are you planning to visit all of these people today?"

"Today and tomorrow."

"I have other work to do, you know."

He flashed me a satisfied grin. "I know. But if you want me to fill you in on any progress I make in the investigation, you'll help me with this."

I realized I could justify charging Brooke for the time I spent driving around with Faulkner. That made me feel better, but I still had other clients who needed attention.

Our second stop was a dental office on Veterans Boulevard. We spent twenty minutes in the waiting room while the doctor finished some unfortunate individual's root canal. After the numb-faced patient had stumbled out the door we introduced ourselves and had a conversation similar to the one with Castillo.

The dentist was five-foot-six, in his fifties, potbellied, and mostly bald. Not the guy I'd seen on Saturday.

We moved on to a Real Estate office on Woodside Road, an Italian restaurant on El Camino Real, and a marketing company in Menlo Park before heading north. No one had any information that would help us, and none of the guys looked like the man I'd seen in Stanley's parking lot.

In Belmont we stopped to visit with the owner of a small circuit board assembly outfit, the owners of a retail boutique, and a Thai restaurant. Again, none of the individuals we interviewed bore any resemblance to the man who had visited Stanley Godard on the day of his death.

It was almost 1:30 by the time we finished talking with the Thai restaurant owner, and I was starving, so I suggested we get some lunch 'to go'. Faulkner didn't argue. We ordered at the counter and took our boxed meals out to the car.

I opened a small box of Spring Rolls and asked, "Who's next?"

Faulkner stuffed a Crab Puff into his mouth and picked up his list.

"Pharmaceutical research firm on Old County Road," he mumbled.

"How many more are we doing today?"

"You getting tired of my company already?"

I chose not to respond to that. Faulkner seemed like a good cop and, in spite of myself, I was starting to like him.

We finished our lunch and he took a cigar out of his pocket. "Do you mind?" he asked, before lighting up.

"No, go ahead." I fished my American Spirit organic cigarettes out of my purse and joined him.

It took us about ten minutes to locate the address on Old County Road. The lot was jammed with cars, but we managed to find a vacant space. It was a warm afternoon and I was sorry to leave the air-conditioned Chevy.

We trudged into the lobby and discovered an unoccupied reception desk with a phone next to a plaque showing instructions on how to contact the employee of your choice. Faulkner lifted the receiver and punched in the extension of the CFO who was listed among Stanley's clients. After a few moments he left a brief voicemail message including his cell number.

Our next stop was an auto body shop, also on Old County Road. We caught one of the employees on the sidewalk taking a cigarette break, and asked him where we could find the owner.

"He's in the paint booth," the man said. "Should be out in a few minutes."

We waited while he finished his smoke. It was another ten minutes before a heavy-set blond man in his late twenties stepped outside.

"Scott Kopelin?" asked Faulkner.

"That's me. What can I do for you?"

Faulkner showed Kopelin his badge and made the introductions, then asked when Kopelin had last seen Stanley and if he'd noticed anything unusual.

"I saw him last week," Kopelin said. "He seemed the same as always. Kind of uptight and nervous, but that wasn't unusual for Stanley. He was a good accountant."

Another dead end, I thought.

"There was one thing," Kopelin continued. "There was this old VW van parked on the street when I went in. I mean *old*, needed bodywork and paint. I notice things like that. Anyway, the motor was running. I didn't think anything about it at first, but it was still there when I came out twenty minutes later and the motor was still running. Engine sounded terrible, like it needed a valve job. I thought maybe the guy was having car trouble, but he was just sitting there in the driver's seat."

Faulkner and I looked at each other. Could this be the same van I had seen before the explosion?

"What color was the van?" I asked.

"Kind of a faded pumpkin-orange, with rust spots," Kopelin said.

Faulkner and I exchanged looks again.

"Did you get a look at the driver?" Faulkner asked.

"Yeah. Mid-thirties, long brown hair, scruffy beard, crazy eyes. I thought about asking him if he needed help until I saw the look in his eyes."

"Did you notice his license plate?" Faulkner asked.

"No. Sorry."

"Would you recognize him if you saw him again?"

"Absolutely."

That was something. I had no idea how the guy in the van fit into the puzzle, but it was too much of a coincidence to ignore. Maybe he was in cahoots with the guy in the Benz.

Faulkner asked Kopelin if he'd be willing to work with a sketch artist and he readily agreed.

After leaving Kopelin's body shop we visited a couple more of Stanley's retail boutique clients, but the owners weren't in. Faulkner left business cards behind, asking that the owners be notified that we would return tomorrow to speak with them.

There were only six men left on the list, including the three we had missed, so we decided to call it a day. Faulkner dropped me off at the marina and I grudgingly agreed to meet him at my office the next morning.

Chapter 11

I hurried down to the boat and hooked a brooding Buddy to his leash. After watering a couple of bushes he stopped sulking and wanted to play. I retrieved one of his tennis balls from my office and noticed that the voicemail light was blinking, but chose to ignore it for the moment. I have my priorities.

Buddy and I played catch on the lawn until he was worn out, then we went into the office where he slurped up half a bowl of water and happily collapsed on the floor.

I turned on the computer and documented the details of my time with Faulkner for the report I would eventually submit to Brooke. When that was done, I pressed the play button on my phone console. The first message was from Jim Sutherland, asking what was happening with the investigation. The second was from Brooke.

"Hi, Nikki. I just got back from my meeting with Stanley's attorney. He's a horrible little man. He all but accused me of being a gold digger. Said it was highly unusual for an *acquaintance* to be the sole beneficiary of an estate such as Stanley's. An *acquaintance.* Can you believe that? I didn't even know Stanley *had* a will! Anyway, call me, please."

As I dialed Brooke's number, I mentally cursed Stanley's attorney for being so tactless. She picked up on the second ring and repeated her story about the "horrible little man." I offered sympathy for her ordeal, and then told her about my day with Faulkner. I described the driver of the van that Kopelin had told us about.

"Have you ever seen anyone like that around Stanley's office?" I asked.

"No, but I've only been to his office three or four times. What are you going to do now?"

"I have to go out with Faulkner again tomorrow morning. We're still hoping to find the client who was with Stanley right before the explosion. After that I'd like to take another look around Stanley's house.

You want to come with me? Maybe we can find whatever they were looking for." Whoever *they* were.

"Okay. But doesn't Detective Faulkner still have the key?"

"I guess he does. Maybe you could call him and ask him to give it to me tomorrow."

"I'll call him right now. Are you in your office?"

"Yes."

"I'll call you back." And she hung up.

While I was waiting to hear back from Brooke, I called Jim and filled him in on the day's activities.

"You think it's the same van?" he asked.

"Of course I do. What I can't figure out is the connection between the guy in the van and the guy driving the Benz."

"Maybe there isn't one."

"You're probably right. Unless the guy in the van is a hit man working for the guy with the Mercedes."

"You read too many mystery novels. Why would a hit man drive such a noticeable car?"

"I don't know. Maybe so people would focus on the car instead of on him."

"Uh huh. And why would this so called hit man's client be in the vicinity right before the murder, do you think?"

"Maybe he didn't know when it was going to happen."

"You're really reaching."

"I know," I sighed. "But I've got nothing, and when I've got nothing, I reach."

My other line rang and I said, "Gotta go."

I answered the incoming call. It was Brooke.

"Detective Faulkner says the crime scene has been released and we can have the house key, but he wants to know if we find anything."

"Of course he does. I'll call you when we finish interviewing Stanley's clients tomorrow."

I ended the call with Brooke and opened my e-mail. I had one from CIS with attachments. I had completely forgotten about the background reports I'd requested on Brooke.

I opened each of the attachments and sent them to the printer. The first one was an invoice. I wrote out a check and addressed an envelope while I waited for everything to finish printing, then I gathered up the pages and began reading.

Brooke had no criminal record in any of the counties I had specified, unless you count the parking ticket she'd received in Palo Alto last year. She had, as she'd told me, grown up and gone to school in North

Carolina, and had earned a Bachelor's degree in marketing from the University of North Carolina. She had moved to California two years ago, after her parents were killed in a car accident. *Fresh start*, I thought.

The financial profile showed a little more than two million in a money market account, and over thirty thousand in checking. She owned her condo and had paid cash for a new VW Jetta. I wondered if Stanley had any idea how well off she was when he'd written his will naming Brooke as the sole beneficiary. Probably not.

Brooke would be relieved to know that there was nothing in any of the reports about her former relationships.

Buddy and I went out and did a couple of early dinner surveys at local restaurants that had patio seating and would allow patrons to bring along well-mannered pets. After leaving him alone on the boat for most of the day I didn't have the heart to lock him in the car.

After completing the surveys we drove back to the marina and I took him for a walk before opening up the office and typing my reports.

We were just boarding the boat when Bill

called. He asked how my day with Faulkner had gone.

"We didn't find the guy, if that's what you mean. I'm going out with him again tomorrow."

"Going out with him?"

Bill is not jealous by nature, but he sometimes pretends to be possessive, and Faulkner *was* good looking.

"Did you eat?" I asked, scooping kibble into Buddy's dish.

"I grabbed a burger on the way home."

"Is that all?"

"Fries, an apple pie, and a chocolate shake."

Bill is one of those men who can eat anything and it magically converts to muscle. I'm not so lucky.

Buddy and I spent the evening cuddled together on the pilothouse settee watching television. Before bed, I took him across the street to the wildlife refuge for a long walk.

We were both completely worn out when we got home. Buddy draped himself across the foot of my bed, and was out like a light. I climbed under the covers and let the gentle sigh of the boat's hull easing up against the fenders lull me to sleep.

CHAPTER 12

FAULKNER KNOCKED ON MY OFFICE door at 8:25 the next morning and Buddy gave a big dog *woof* as he stepped inside.

"I hope you like dogs," I said. "This is Buddy. He'll be coming with us today."

Faulkner looked apprehensive, but he slowly squatted down and presented the back of his hand to Buddy, who sniffed and then licked it. After receiving Buddy's seal of approval, Faulkner seated himself in one of my visitor's chairs and handed me a large manila envelope.

"Autopsy report," he said.

"Is this my copy?"

"You can read it, but you can't keep it."

So I read it, slowly and carefully. Stanley Godard's cause of death was a .38 caliber bullet wound to the head. The ME had also determined that he had been close to the center of the explosion. I thought about that. Why blow up the office if Stanley was already dead? What might the killer have hoped to accomplish? All of Stanley's hard copy records had been burned to a crisp and his computer seriously damaged. Maybe there was something incriminating in the records.

When I had read every word and taken copious notes, I slid the report back into the envelope, which I handed to Faulkner.

"Why do you think they blew up the office if Stanley was already dead?" I asked.

"I'll ask the killer when I find him." He took a smaller envelope out of his pocket and handed it to me. "I need you to sign for this."

I opened the envelope. Inside was the key to Stanley's house. I signed the receipt form that Faulkner put in front of me and slipped the key envelope into my purse. We went out to Faulkner's car, and Buddy jumped in the back seat without any prompting from me. What a good boy. Our first stop today was the pharmaceutical research firm on Old County Road where we had missed the CFO yesterday. Once again the parking lot was full. As we cruised slowly around looking for an empty space I spotted a shiny new silver Mercedes.

"Stop!" I shouted, alarming Faulkner, who slammed on the brakes causing Buddy to skid forward into the back of his seat.

"*What?*" Faulkner snapped at me.

"That Benz," I said, pointing. "It's just like the one I saw in Stanley's parking lot."

Faulkner and I stared at the dealership logo in the license plate holder. I got out of the car and took a closer look. It was a model C350 Plug-In Hybrid, and it was locked, but at least now we knew where it had been purchased.

I got back into the Chevy and turned to Faulkner. "Can you have it booted?"

"No probable cause," he said.

"Don't you ever bend the rules?"

"I try not to."

Once we found a parking space, Buddy and I stood near the Benz while Faulkner went inside. The plan was that he would bring the CFO outside with him. Faulkner was back five minutes later, and he was alone.

"Let me guess. You got his voicemail again."

"Yep."

"Can you get a uniform to sit on this car until the owner comes out?"

"Inappropriate use of manpower. We don't even know if it's the same car."

"*Christ*, Faulkner. What's the CFO's name?"

We were back in the Chevy and Faulkner started the engine and turned up the AC before handing me the list of names. I found the entry and read the name out loud. "Geoffrey Archer." An easy name to remember.

We drove to one of the boutiques in San Carlos that we had visited the day before, and Faulkner left the engine running so Buddy and I wouldn't roast. I pulled out my notebook and wrote down *Geoffrey Archer.* My plan was to Google the name and see if I could find a home address or a photo. If that didn't work, I'd come back and wait in the parking lot until the guy came out at the end of the day.

I tucked the notebook back in my purse and looked up as Faulkner approached with a tall man in tow. I got out of the car and Faulkner introduced me to Albert Charles, the boutique owner. He was about the same height, weight, and age as the man I'd seen on Saturday, but his artfully layered hair was dyed an unnatural shade of red, and his features were soft, in fact his whole body looked soft. Not the same guy.

Faulkner asked the obligatory questions, but we didn't learn anything new.

We met the last of Stanley's male clients before noon, leaving only Archer the CFO. I was convinced he was the one. He hadn't returned Faulkner's calls, he wasn't answering his phone, and the silver Mercedes cinched it.

Faulkner dropped me and Buddy off at the marina. He thanked me for my time and I thanked him for showing me the autopsy report. Neither of us mentioned Archer.

After walking Buddy, I unlocked the office, splashed some cold water on my face, tossed some ice cubes in Buddy's water dish, and turned on the computer. I did a Google search for Geoffrey Archer in San Carlos, and got three hits linking him to the research firm. One was a newspaper article announcing his appointment to CFO, but there was no photograph.

I pulled up the online white pages and found several Archers listed in the San Francisco Bay area, but no Geoffreys.

I called Brooke and asked if we could search Stanley's house tomorrow. I didn't want to risk missing something because I was in a hurry, and I needed to be back in San Carlos before Archer left his office for the day. Brooke said that would be fine. She'd taken the week off from work, and her cousin Robbyn was flying in this afternoon. I was happy to hear that. She needed to be around someone who cared about her right now.

Buddy and I did three lunch surveys. It took me longer to find shady parking spots than it took to do the actual reports. Of course I was rushing, not wanting to leave him in the car when it was this hot outside.

At 4:25 we drove back to San Carlos and I parked under a tree at the edge of the research company lot. I cranked up the air conditioning for a few minutes, then lowered the windows halfway and shut off the engine. Buddy gave me a mournful look as I got out of the car.

"I'll be back soon," I assured him.

I zigzagged between parked cars, making my way to the Benz. Halfway across the lot I spotted Faulkner standing next to an SUV a few spaces away from the Mercedes, puffing on a stogie. He smiled when he saw me approaching.

"Thought I might see you here," he said.

"It's my civic duty." I grinned back at him. "How long have you been waiting?"

"Half an hour."

By 5:30 the lot was more than half empty, and still no sign of Archer. I walked back to my car and hooked Buddy to his leash, got him out of the car, and let him water some trees and bushes at the periphery of the lot, all the while keeping an eye on the Mercedes.

I took a watcr bottle out of my purse and gave Buddy a long drink, then asked him to get back into the car. He just stared at me. I was thinking about moving my car closer to the Benz so I could leave the windows all the way down for Buddy when I turned back toward the building and saw Archer coming out a side door. Adrenaline shot through my system. I slammed the car door and Buddy and I took off running. Faulkner had seen Archer too, but more importantly Archer had seen Faulkner who, even in plain clothes, looked like a cop.

Archer stopped in his tracks. He looked panicky. Then his expression changed, as though he had come to a decision. He was going to run. I could feel it. He turned back toward the door, but it had closed and locked behind him. He fished in his pocket for the keys, glancing over his shoulder at Faulkner, trying to act casual.

"Mr. Archer?" Faulkner called out.

Archer ignored him. He was trying to get the key into the lock. Buddy and I raced past Faulkner who was moving more slowly toward the building. We were only a few yards away when Archer pushed the door open and stepped inside.

"Stop!" I shouted, and launched myself through the entryway to keep the door from closing, accidentally tackling Archer in the process. He was a big man, but I had momentum on my side and I knocked him to his knees. I scrambled up and planted my size ten shoe against the door so Faulkner could get in behind us. I drew the Ruger from my fanny pack holster, pointed the muzzle at Archer, and said, "Don't move a muscle."

Buddy growled deep in his throat as Faulkner came through the door.

"What the hell to you think you're doing?" Faulkner asked.

"This is *him*!" I said, trying to catch my breath. "This is the guy I saw in the parking lot before the explosion."

"You wanna holster that thing before somebody gets hurt?"

I stepped away from Archer, who struggled to his feet. Buddy's growl increased in volume and Archer huddled against the wall.

I stroked Buddy's head and said, "Good dog."

"Are you Geoffrey Archer?" Faulkner asked.

Archer nodded.

"I'm Detective Faulkner." He showed Archer his badge. "And this is Ms. Hunter. We'd like to ask you some questions about your association with Stanley Godard."

Archer flinched at the name.

"Can we do this someplace else?" he whimpered.

There were tears in his eyes. I thought it might be guilt or remorse, but maybe he'd banged his knees on the concrete when I'd knocked him down. Hard to tell.

Faulkner took hold of Archer's arm just above the elbow and said, "You can ride with me to the police department."

Once Archer was locked in the backseat of the Chevy, Faulkner turned to me, a grim look on his face. "Are you fucking nuts?" he hissed. "He could file assault charges."

"He could have gotten away too, and you're welcome. I'll meet you at the station." As I turned on my heel I caught the shadow of a grin on Faulkner's face.

CHAPTER 13

I BROKE THE SPEED LIMIT GETTING to the San Carlos PD. I wanted to arrive before Faulkner did, find a shady spot to park Buddy, and catch Faulkner before he entered the building, so he'd have to let me sit in on the interview. I had a feeling he'd try to ditch me now that I'd served my purpose by identifying his suspect.

The SCPD is located on Elm Street and is flanked on one side by the library and on the other by a public park. I drove into the underground lot, lowered the windows part way, and locked my fanny pack with the Ruger in the trunk. I jogged up to the street just as the Chevy made the turn into the Police Department complex. I waved frantically, trying to get Faulkner's attention. He spotted me, stopped the car, and waited.

I jumped into the front passenger seat and Faulkner pulled the car into a reserved space near the back of the building. He turned to me before getting out of the car.

"We need to talk. But first I need to get Mr. Archer secured in an interview room. You can wait for me in the lobby." His tone didn't leave any room for discussion.

Faulkner had a firm grip on Archer as he marched him into the building, but I followed close behind, just in case Archer tried to make another run for it. Faulkner escorted him through a door that had to be buzzed open, and I perched on the edge of a chair in the lobby. I was dying for a cigarette, but the possibility of missing out on the interview outweighed my craving for nicotine.

Faulkner came back to the lobby and stood holding the security door open while I grabbed my purse and hustled inside. When the door had closed behind us he said, "I'm going to let you observe, but you can't be in the room with me."

"Wait a minute. You wouldn't even have known about this guy if it weren't for me. I have a right to ask him some questions."

"No, you don't. I can put you in the

observation room, but that's the best I can do. Take it or leave it."

"Fine," I huffed. "I'll take it."

He walked me down the hall and showed me into a tiny room with four monitors mounted above a table. He fiddled with a remote and one of the monitors came to life. I saw Archer seated in a small room, his head in his hands. Faulkner did something else with the remote and I heard a scraping sound as Archer pushed back his chair and stood up. He began pacing, looked out the window, turned unhappily toward the locked door, and then sat down again.

"Stay here," Faulkner said. "I'll come and get you when I'm done."

The small room smelled of Lysol and made me feel mildly claustrophobic, but I quickly forgot about the confining space when Faulkner entered the interview room. He seated himself across from Archer, took a notebook out of his pocket, and asked, "How long were you a client of Stanley Godard's?"

"Not long," said Archer. "Maybe two weeks. He was conducting an audit for my firm."

"Why did you go to see him on Saturday morning?"

"He'd asked for some invoice and check copies. I was bringing them to him."

"What happened while you were in his office?"

"I gave him the copies. He was looking them over when someone knocked on the back door. He looked surprised, but he got up and went to answer the door. He was only gone for a few seconds when I heard a shot."

"A gunshot?"

"Yes."

"How did you know it was a gunshot?"

"I've done some hunting. I know what a gun sounds like, and I smelled the cordite."

"Do you own a thirty-eight caliber handgun Mr. Archer?"

"No."

"Okay. You heard a gunshot. Then what happened?"

"I ran out the front door."

"Did you see anyone else in the office?"

"No. I didn't hang around to see who had fired the gun. I just ran."

I didn't know if I believed Archer or not, but his story made sense in terms of the timing of what I had observed. Of course the timing also worked if *he'd* been the one who shot Stanley.

"Why didn't you call the police?" Faulkner asked.

"I didn't want to get involved. Then I saw on the news that Godard was dead, and I was afraid if I came forward the killer would come after me too. I hadn't seen anything anyway. I knew I couldn't help."

"What was in the suitcase you brought into the office with you?" Faulkner asked.

"Suitcase?" Archer said, adjusting the knot of his tie.

"You were seen carrying a small suitcase into the office, Mr. Archer. When you ran back outside, you no longer had the suitcase with you. What was in it?"

"Maybe I should call my attorney."

"You have that right," Faulkner said. He pushed a telephone across the table toward Archer. "Would you like some privacy?"

"Yes, please."

Faulkner got up and left the room. Moments later he came into the room where I was seated and turned off the monitor.

"What are you doing?" I asked. "I want to hear what he says to his attorney."

"He's legally entitled to a private conversation with his lawyer."

"*Jesus*, Faulkner! What are you, a boy scout?"

Faulkner seemed unperturbed by my

verbal assault. "You might as well go home. Now that he's asked for his attorney, we probably won't get anything more out of him. He's not under arrest, so he doesn't have to talk to me. His attorney will know that. He may have something to hide, but I don't think he killed your client's fiancé."

"Why not?"

"Instinct. He doesn't strike me as the type. For one thing, I don't think he's got the balls."

"Cowards sometimes kill to protect themselves. You said yourself he's hiding something. I'll stick around if it's all the same to you."

"What about your dog? This could take a while."

He had me there. I didn't like leaving Buddy in the car.

"I'll take him home and then come back. What's your cell number?"

"Look, I've already stretched the rules by allowing you to listen in on the interview. Go home. I'll call you later."

I reluctantly allowed Faulkner to escort me to the lobby. As I crossed to the door he said, "Thanks for your help with this."

I waved at him over my shoulder, not

bothering to turn around, and pushed my way outside.

Buddy was sulking, again, when I unlocked the car, so I took him for a long walk around the park before driving back to the marina.

CHAPTER 14

I WAS WASHING MY DINNER DISHES when the cell phone in my pocket started vibrating. I'd been hoping for a call from Faulkner.

"Hunter Investigations," I answered.

"He didn't do it," Faulkner said without preamble.

"And you know this because..."

"According to Archer's attorney, he had nothing but invoice and check copies in the suitcase. He said Godard needed them before he would sign off on the audit. Apparently he was being a real hard-ass about it."

"And you believe him? Why did Archer need a suitcase just to carry some invoice and check copies? And why couldn't he tell you that without his attorney present?"

"Maybe there were a lot of them? I don't know."

"Did you ask him about the guy in the van?"

"No. I need to find him first, in case he and Archer are in this together. Maybe then I can get one of them to roll on the other."

"You said you didn't think Archer was a killer."

"That doesn't mean he didn't hire someone to kill for him."

Huh, I thought, *maybe my theory wasn't so far-fetched after all.*

I ended the call with Faulkner and dialed Brooke's home number. An unfamiliar female voice answered.

"Evans residence," the voice said in a honeyed Southern accent.

"Is this Robbyn?" I asked.

"Yes. Who's this?"

"Nikki Hunter. Is Brooke there?"

"Oh, you're the lady PI she told me about. Hang on a sec."

Brooke came on the line and I told her about the latest development in the case.

She listened silently, and then asked, "Is your friend still following me?"

"You mean Jim? I don't think so. Why?"

"I'm probably being silly, but when I went to the airport to pick Robbyn up I had this creepy feeling that I was being watched."

I knew that feeling. "Did you see anyone?"

"You know how crowded the airport is," she sighed.

"Let me call Jim and I'll call you right back. Is your door locked?"

"Yes."

I called Jim Sutherland on his cell.

"What's up Nikki?"

"Have you or any of your operatives been shadowing Brooke Evans?"

"Not since Friday night. Why?"

"She's pretty sure she's being followed."

"Uh oh."

"Yeah. Maybe whoever killed Stanley and searched his house thinks Brooke has what he, or she, was looking for."

"Did she take anything from the house?"

"Just Stanley's orchid journal."

"Have you looked at the journal?"

"Not yet."

"Didn't you tell me one of Stanley's orchids was stolen?"

"The hybrid, yeah."

"So maybe our killer is into orchids. I suggest you take a look at that journal as soon as possible."

"Good idea."

I ended the call with Jim and called Brooke back. I told her that he hadn't been tailing her.

"What did you do with Stanley's journal?" I asked.

"I put it in my safe deposit box. Whoever took the hybrid was probably looking for the journal. Without Stanley's data on the hybridization method the plant will be worthless. It's one of a kind. If it was another grower who took it, they'll never be able to duplicate the process."

"Why didn't you mention that to me before?" I asked, trying to keep the frustration out of my voice.

"I don't know. I guess I was upset. Do you think whoever took the orchid is the person who killed Stanley?"

"Well, it did happen on the same day."

You'd have to be insane to kill someone over a plant, I thought.

"Brooke, is the missing orchid worth anything?"

"You mean money?"

"Yes."

"I'm not sure. It would be priceless to a hybridizer. Stanley said that once he introduced it at the conference his name would become legend in the orchid community."

"Would you recognize the orchid if you saw it again?"

"I'm not sure. I'd recognize the pot."

"They could change the pot. What color was the bud?"

"It was kind of a silvery blue."

"Wow."

I was thinking that if Faulkner failed to find the VW guy, Brooke and I might have to attend the orchid conference.

"Nikki? Are you still there?"

"I'm here. How long is Robbyn going to be in town?"

"Till Sunday."

"Make sure you stay together. Are you going out tonight?"

"We were planning to go out for dinner. You think that's a bad idea?"

"I do. Better safe than sorry. I'll come by in the morning and I think either Jim or I should be with you at all times until this guy is caught. Is that okay with you?"

"Sure. What does Jim look like?"

"He's a tall red-head. If he isn't available to come himself, I'll get a description of the agent he's sending and call you back."

"Okay. Thank you, Nikki."

"Brooke, there's something else. Before all this happened, I was thinking about having you take a late night drive to flush out anyone Stanley might have had following you. It might speed things up if we did that now, but the risk has increased. Plus, we don't know for sure that you're being followed and, if you are, we don't know what your stalker is after. I'm just thinking out loud here, but what if you get the journal out of your safe deposit box and make a show of taking it back to your condo. Then I could wait inside while you and Robbyn go out again."

"I'm all for speeding things up, but that sounds dangerous."

"Jim can follow you to and from the bank."

"No, I mean it sounds like it will be dangerous for *you*."

I was growing fond of Brooke. Not many people show concern for their personal bodyguard.

"I'll be okay," I said.

I knew I needed to tell Faulkner what I was doing, but I thought maybe I'd put that conversation off for a day or two.

I called Jim and told him I needed someone at Brooke's condo complex tonight.

"I'll go," he said without hesitation.

I told him about the plan to get the journal from the bank tomorrow, and that if we didn't flush the killer out using the journal as bait, we might have to attend the orchid conference where Brooke had said Stanley was going to reveal his new hybrid.

"If the killer is the same person who took Stanley's orchid, he'll probably be at that conference."

"You really think someone would kill for an orchid?"

"It's a very unique hybrid. Brooke is the only other person who's seen it, and she's not sure she could identify it if it's in a different pot. I'm going up to the office for a little while. I need to do some research. Call me if anything happens?"

"Will do."

I walked Buddy, then brought him into the office with me.

I turned on the computer, opened a web browser, Googled *Santa Barbara International Orchid Show*, and selected the link to the conference website. The event was being held at the Earl Warren Showgrounds from March 4th through the 6th. Today was March 1st, so the 4th was Friday, only three days away. Not a lot of time to plan for a road trip to Santa Barbara. I surfed around a little and found a link for *exhibitor registration*. There was a note saying space was limited and encouraging exhibitors to sign up early.

I spotted the *contact us* link, clicked on that, and got a list of e-mail addresses. I selected the one for registration and typed a brief e-mail saying I was a freelance journalist in Redwood City, writing an article about the upcoming event. I wanted to interview growers in the San Francisco Bay Area who were planning to introduce new hybrids at the conference, and I hoped they could provide me with the names of those who had registered.

There were no phone numbers posted on the website, but if I didn't get a prompt response to my e-mail, I'd try to find a local chapter of the American Orchid Society, maybe attend a meeting and see if anyone turned up in an old VW van.

I shut down the computer and locked up the office, then took Buddy for another walk. We ended up at the point, at the end of the marina parking lot, staring out at the bay. It was a gorgeous evening, the sky clear and full of stars, and I almost felt guilty for enjoying it, considering what Brooke was going through. Almost, but not quite.

CHAPTER 15

WEDNESDAY MORNING I WAS UP early. I guzzled coffee from a thermal mug while I walked Buddy, and then hit the gym for my lower body workout. After I'd showered and dressed I called Brooke at home.

"I'm on my way," I said. "But I wanted to make sure it was okay to bring my dog, Buddy, along. Are pets allowed in your building?"

"Oh, yes. Several of the tenants have dogs. Is he... um... well behaved?"

I knew she was asking if Buddy was likely to soil her carpet. I stifled my indignation and said, "Very."

When I arrived at the complex I parked next to a silver Honda Civic with tinted windows. As I got out of my car the driver's side window of the Civic lowered a few inches and Jim's bloodshot eyes stared out at me.

"Have you been here all night?" I asked.

"Yup."

"Are you good for a couple more hours?" I told him what I had in mind for this morning.

"I'm fine," he said, reaching for a thermos of coffee.

Lengthy stakeouts are easier for men because they can pee in a cup when necessary. Knowing that made me feel a little less guilty.

"I'll call you when Brooke and Robbyn are ready to leave. Stay close to them."

"No problem," he said, and raised the window.

Buddy and I knocked on Brooke's door, which was opened by a slender, blonde woman in her thirties who could have been Brooke's twin, except that she was slightly less muscular. I wondered about the genetic background of the Evans family. Were they all this stunning?

The woman shook my hand and said, "You must be Nikki. I'm Robbyn." Without waiting for an answer she bent down and crooned, "And you must be *Buddy.* Aren't *you* a handsome boy?" She ruffled his ears and Buddy grinned, wagged his tail, and licked her cheek.

Brooke came in from the kitchen, drying her hands on a dishtowel. "I see y'all have met. Would you like some coffee, Nikki?"

"I'd love some, thanks."

Before pouring the coffee, Brooke handed me a black and white drawing of a man with long hair and a beard. "That's the identikit picture of the man driving the van," she said. "Detective Faulkner dropped it off last night. He said I should be on the lookout for this man, and if I see him I should go someplace crowded and call him immediately."

"Sounds like good advice."

I studied the picture. The identikit artist had captured the eyes that Kopelin had described to me and Faulkner on Monday. This guy had some serious crazy going on.

The three of us huddled around the kitchen counter and discussed my plan. At 10:00 Brooke and Robbyn would go to the bank and get Stanley's journal out of the safe deposit box. Jim would follow. Walking from the bank back to her car, Brooke would wave the journal around and make a show of discussing it with Robbyn. They would drive slowly back to the condo complex, display the journal again for anyone who was watching when they arrived, then come inside and leave the journal with me. After a few minutes they'd leave again. Buddy and I would wait in the apartment, hoping someone would try to break in and steal the journal.

The only flaw in the plan was Buddy. I couldn't leave him home alone again, or lock him in the car, but he's not always good at being quiet. If someone tried to break into Brooke's condo, Buddy would probably go into protective mode and bark, and the thief would bolt. Then I'd have another chase scene on my hands. I was still a little stiff from tackling Archer yesterday. Of course, I could just shoot the guy in the ass as he was running away. That would slow him down.

At 9:55 I called Jim on his cell and told him Brooke and Robbyn were coming out. He was parked near enough to Brooke's Jetta that he wouldn't need to move his car to cover them.

We had decided to leave the deadbolt unlocked in order to facilitate my plan, so after they left Buddy and I sat in the living room watching the front door.

Thirty minutes later Jim called to tell me they were back. I heard a key in the lock and Buddy barked one time as the door opened, before he saw Brooke and Robbyn. Then he started wagging. Brooke handed me the journal.

"Lock the deadbolt please," I said. "Did you see anyone following you?"

"We didn't even see *Jim.*"

"He's good."

I called Jim before they went back out, and stayed on the line with him until I knew Brooke and Robbyn were safely in Brooke's car.

"Have you seen anyone suspicious?" I asked.

"Not yet."

"How are you holding up?"

"I'm okay."

"If he doesn't come after the journal in the next hour or so, I think we can assume he isn't watching."

"Sounds good. Talk to you later."

Brooke and Robbyn were going to do some clothes shopping at Neiman's, where Robbyn intended to take full advantage of Brooke's employee discount. I was only a little bit envious. Jim would keep an eye on the two women from a discreet distance.

I filled a bowl with water for Buddy, set my Ruger on the coffee table, and opened the journal. Stanley's handwriting was precise and easy to read. I scanned the pages leading up to February and then began reading the details. Unfortunately, everything in the journal related to his work on the orchid hybridization process. There was nothing about other members of the orchid club who might have been jealous of his recent success.

By 11:30 I was bored with the journal and convinced the killer had missed Brooke's performance this morning. I'd have to think of another way to get his attention, assuming Stanley had been killed for his hybrid. I still had my doubts about that. If Archer had been skimming funds from his employer, and Stanley had been onto him, then Archer had a strong motive. It crossed my mind that Stanley might not have been above blackmailing Archer. I was contemplating the possibilities when my cell phone vibrated in my pocket.

"Any luck?" asked Jim.

"Nothing."

"The girls are done shopping. They want to stop for lunch before we head back. Is that okay with you?"

"Sure. It doesn't look like our guy's going to try anything today."

We disconnected and I looked down at Buddy. "What do you think? Was Stanley killed for his new breed of orchid or because he knew too much about Archer?"

Buddy chuffed noiselessly. Probably a Rhodesian Ridgeback trait. He only barks out loud when he perceives a threat.

Since there was nothing happening with the case, I took a tour of Brooke's condo. Everything was neat as a pin, including the huge master bathroom. I took in the double sinks, overhead sunlamp, and expensive assortment of treatment creams and lotions on the vanity counter. Brooke favored Chantecaille "Pure Rosewater" toner, La Mer "The Hand Treatment," Lancome "Progres Eye" cream, Laura Mercier "Flawless Skin Repair Day Crème," Clarins "Super Restorative Night" cream, and Palmer's "Cocoa Butter Firming Butter" body lotion. That last one didn't look like something you'd purchase at Neiman's, but what do I know. I went back to the living room and grabbed the notebook I carry everywhere, then copied down the names of all six products. Brooke's radiant complexion was probably inherited, but I love trying new things.

At 12:45 my cell vibrated again. I

assumed it was Jim, calling to tell me they were on their way, so I didn't bother checking the display.

"Hunter."

"Nikki, it's Bill. I have bad news."

"Are you okay?"

"I'm fine, but I just caught a homicide. The victim, Nick Lawrence, was killed at his home in Westport. Weapon was a knife coated with garlic extract."

"Oh *shit.* Nina's back," I said, my blood running cold. What I didn't say was that Westport was right next to Redwood Shores, where I was sitting at this very moment. Could there *be* more of a coincidence?

Chapter 16

Nina Jezek was a notorious multiple murderer of pedophiles and the miscreants who engage in child trafficking for the purpose of sexual exploitation. Her M.O. is killing with a stiletto coated with garlic, which prevents blood from coagulating. We'd met briefly two months ago when I was hired by the nine-year-old son of one of her victims. The last I'd heard, she was on a killing spree in Europe, leaving me to assume that Nina would be Interpol's problem until she was caught. I had tried to put her out of my mind.

"Nikki?" Bill said.

"Yeah, I'm still here."

"I thought you'd want to know."

"Thanks. Was the victim a known sex offender?"

"The FBI says he was associated with Alfredo Giordano, who was suspected of being a supplier of… you know… children."

Alfredo "The Tongue" Giordano had been killed at his home in the Woodside Hills last December. Jim Sutherland and I had been watching Nina that night, and I'd followed her to Giordano's house. After his body had been found, Bill had mentioned that Giordano had been on the FBI's Violent Crimes Against Children watch list because he was suspected of child trafficking. That, of course, was also why Giordano had been on Nina's list.

"How does someone even get into that line of work?" I asked.

It was a rhetorical question and Bill didn't respond.

"Any witnesses?" I asked.

"Not that we know of. Lawrence was found by his admin assistant this morning. She went to his house when he didn't show up at the office, and found his body in the garage. When I arrived at the scene the blood had already dried, but I could still smell the garlic, so I put a rush on the autopsy. Coroner says he was killed between four and nine p.m. yesterday."

"You think I need to worry?"

"You mean do I think Nina will come after you?"

"Yeah."

"That wouldn't be her style. You caught her in the act, and because of you she had to leave the country, but you're not a sex offender, so no, I don't think you need to worry. Besides she had the chance to kill you that night in Los Altos, and didn't."

"That's not very reassuring. Scott's mom wasn't a sex offender either, and Nina killed her."

"I gotta go. I'll be working late tonight."

I found myself struggling with the same jumble of emotions I'd experienced during the investigation that had led me to Nina Jezek in the first place. She was a stone-cold killer and had to be stopped, but her victims preyed on innocent children and the world was better off without them.

Nina's only non-sex offender victim had been Gloria Freedman. She had verbally abused and beaten her young son, but he had loved her anyway. When she was murdered he'd hired me to find her killer. Scott was now living in Seattle with his great uncle, J.V. Trusty. A fellow PI as well as a musician, J.V. is wonderful with Scott. They're lucky to have each other. I would have to let him know that Nina was back in the U.S., and ask if he and Scott wanted to hire me again to apprehend her.

My cell phone vibrated and I answered, feeling distracted by the past.

"We're here," said Jim. "Any action?"

"No, but Nina's back in town."

Jim had helped me with Scott's case, so he knew all about Nina Jezek.

"Shit," he said. "I thought she was gone for good."

"No such luck."

Chapter 17

Nina Jezek's flight from Tijuana had touched down at SFO right on schedule. She'd made her way through customs without a hitch, and caught a cab outside the international terminal. The cabbie dropped her off at the Hyatt House in Belmont near Redwood Shores, where she had booked a suite for the week under her current alias, Sandra Ellis. She'd also been able to rent a car at the hotel, but, in fact, she could have walked to her first target's home.

Her appearance had changed since she'd last been in the United States. Her hair was longer and now a warm shade of honey-blonde. Her fingerprints had been permanently removed with acid, and she wore brown contact lenses to conceal the intense blue of her eyes. She'd also had her nose and cheekbones widened.

Nina had spent a few days observing her next target before taking action. She'd become familiar with his schedule, the routes he normally drove to and from his office, and the restaurants he favored. She knew gaining access to his home would be problematic. Since he preferred the company of little girls, she would be unable to charm her way into his confidence. The house also had a state-of-the-art alarm system, which was beyond her breaking and entering capabilities.

The only chink in Nick Lawrence's armor was that he didn't like cleaning his own home, and allowed a housekeeping service access to the first and second floors once a week. She'd sat in her rental car watching as the van approached his residence on Tuesday morning. Lawrence had opened the garage door and was leaving for the office just as the cleaning crew finished unloading their supplies. He acknowledged the crew supervisor with a nod, and left the overhead door open after pulling his car out onto the street.

The uniformed maintenance crew entered the house through the garage. Nina smiled. This could work. All she had to do was slip into the garage and conceal herself until the cleaning service employees were gone.

She waited until all the supplies had been carried into the house, then left the safety of her car and casually strolled up the driveway.

CHAPTER 18

THIRTY SECONDS AFTER JIM AND I disconnected Brooke and Robbyn came through the door carrying Neiman Marcus shopping bags, which Buddy nuzzled hoping for a treat.

"What did you buy?" I asked, unable to resist.

Robbyn had purchased only clothes she could wear in the classroom, but they were elegant. A lime green cashmere shell and matching cardigan, a pair of taupe Capri pants, and enough lacy pastel lingerie to last a lifetime.

Brooke had bought herself a new Dooney & Bourke clutch. I've never been able to fit everything I need into a clutch, which is why I favor oversized crossbody bags.

"You mind if I hang on to this for a few days?" I asked, holding up the journal.

"I guess not, if you think it will help."

"I'll carry it around with me and hope the orchid thief is watching. Maybe he'll come after me instead of you. Are you two up for a visit to Stanley's house?"

Brooke looked at me and blinked a couple of times, then said, "I'd totally forgotten you wanted to do that today. Just let me change clothes. I'd like to tidy up the house while you're searching." She turned to Robbyn. "You don't have to come if you're too tired from all the shopping."

"I wouldn't miss it. Besides, I can help you clean."

They went into the bedroom to change clothes.

I called Jim and told him he could go home.

"You want me back here tonight?"

"Yes, please. Or one of your agents."

"I don't have anything more urgent going on. What time?"

"Nine would be good. Thank you, Jim."

Both women changed into spandex shorts, cotton tank tops, and athletic shoes. They looked like they belonged on the cover of a fitness magazine. We all trooped down to the parking lot. Buddy watered a few bushes, then he and I climbed into the BMW and followed Brooke's Jetta to Belmont.

I parked on the street outside Stanley's house and hooked Buddy to his leash. We walked him around the backyard so he could get a scent-related feel for the place, then I unlocked the back door and handed Brooke the key.

We went in through the kitchen and I searched the cabinets for a bowl large enough to fill with water for the pup while Brooke assembled Stanley's cleaning supplies on the kitchen counter. I found a large Tupper and filled it at the sink. Buddy drained the dish, so I refilled it and set it in the corner of the room.

"I'm going to look around upstairs," I said.

Brooke was pulling on a pair of pink Playtex gloves. "Okay," she said.

As an afterthought, I walked to the back door and threw the deadbolt.

Buddy followed me up to the second floor and into Stanley's bedroom. I stood in the middle of the room taking in my surroundings, wondering where I would hide something if I had OCD. I thought about what Brooke had said about Stanley—

that he documented everything. If he'd had reason to believe that Archer, or someone at his firm, was involved in criminal activity, would he have kept the evidence at the office, or might he have brought a copy home?

As I searched Stanley's bedroom I tried to think like Adrian Monk, my favorite OCD TV detective. Monk's character had a lot in common with Stanley Godard. Everything had its place. Probably the 'place' for client information was at his office.

All of Stanley's jacket and pants pockets were empty, as were his shoes. Nothing had been sewn into the lining of his clothes or his drapes. There was nothing under any of his bedroom furniture, not even dust bunnies.

There were a couple of watercolor landscapes on the bedroom walls, but nothing was hidden behind them. The wooden floor panels were all secure and the closet walls were stucco; nothing hidden there. The closet ceiling had an access panel leading up to the crawl space between the ceiling and the roof, so I pulled a straight backed chair into the closet and stood on it, pushed up the panel, and turned on my cell phone flashlight. There was a thin layer of dust, but nothing was stored up there.

I replaced the panel and the chair, and

moved into the guest bedroom, with the same lack of results.

Stanley's bathroom was spotless. His medicine cabinet contained only toothpaste, a toothbrush, dental floss, a comb, a single wrapped bar of unscented Dial soap, and a bottle of generic buffered aspirin. The cabinet under the sink held cleaning supplies, a six-pack of Angel Soft toilet tissue, and a roll of Bounty paper towels. The shower yielded only shampoo and soap. I was getting nowhere.

Buddy and I went downstairs and looked in on Brooke and Robbyn before moving on to Stanley's home office. They were still busy scouring the kitchen.

Brooke looked up as I stepped into the doorway. "Find anything?" she asked.

"Nothing yet. Did Stanley ever mention having a safe in the house?"

She thought for a moment. "No, but I think he had one at the office."

I pulled out my cell and called Faulkner. When he picked up, I said, "Did you find a safe in the remains of Stanley's office?"

"And hello to you too," he said. "I haven't been back to the office since Sunday, and I didn't see a safe, but there was so much charred rubble it might have been buried."

"Brooke thinks there was a safe."

"I'll go take a look."

"Call me back?"

"Sure."

I resumed my search, wondering what secrets the safe might hold. Maybe evidence enough to get an arrest warrant for Archer, if not for homicide at least for embezzling.

There wasn't much of interest in Stanley's home office. I found his personal tax returns and banking records, a copy of his will, the deed to his house, and a copy of his life insurance policy. Brooke had been listed as the beneficiary on an addendum filed only a month ago. She would be receiving a payout of two hundred and fifty thousand dollars. I looked through the books on Stanley's shelves and checked under the desk, under the desk chair, and under all the drawers.

When Buddy and I came out of the office, Brooke and Robbyn were in the living room shelving books and straightening couch cushions. Brooke had brought out Stanley's vacuum cleaner. Buddy sniffed at the Hoover suspiciously. Buddy hates vacuum cleaners. On the boat I use a compact little Dirt Devil, and he barks nonstop until I turn the thing off again.

We went through the living room

together, tidying up as we searched, but there was no secret stash of incriminating documents. When Brooke plugged the vacuum into a wall socket I decided Buddy and I should go outside for a smoke.

Since the yard was fenced I didn't bother to hook the pup to his leash, but I did unzip the fanny pack holster so I would have easy access to my Ruger. Buddy sniffed around the border of the greenhouse as I lit up. He watered a few shrubs, then went back to the greenhouse door and sniffed at the ground. I noticed his hackles were raised and stepped closer.

"What's wrong, Buddy?" He looked up at me and wagged uncertainly. "Do you smell something bad?"

I wondered if he could pick up the scent of the orchid thief and if insanity had an odor that was discernable to dogs. I decided to take another look around the greenhouse, even though the crime scene guys had already been in there. There was probably still glass on the interior floor from the broken pane in the door, so I told Buddy to sit and stay. I crushed out my cigarette on the brick walkway, reached through the hole, and opened the door. I glanced back at Buddy, making sure he wasn't planning to follow me, then stepped inside, closing the door behind me.

The inside of the greenhouse was like a furnace. There was black fingerprint dust on the surface of the table near where the hybrid orchid had been, but everything else looked pretty much as it had on Sunday.

I let my eyes roam over the tables arrayed with what were no doubt prize-winning orchids. Maybe I should water them. I looked around and found a large watering can in the corner. It was full, so I made the rounds of the tables, giving each orchid a little drink. When I reached the end of the center table my eye was caught by a ray of sunlight shining through the glass ceiling and spotlighting a long, wavy, light brown hair that was trapped between two planks. I leaned closer and saw that the hair had a split end.

I hurried outside, securing the door behind me again, and ran into the house. I rifled through the kitchen drawers, found a small zip-lock bag, and rushed back out to the greenhouse.

"Good dog," I said, as I slipped past Buddy.

I carefully freed the hair from the table, placing it inside the baggie and zipping it shut. There was a tiny tear-shaped bulb at the root end. Even if the thief had worn gloves, now we would have his, or her, DNA.

I stepped back outside and called Faulkner on my cell.

"I found the safe," he said, having recognized my number on his display. "We'll move it to the station and get someone to open it for us. I'll let you know if we find anything interesting."

"That's great, but it's not why I called. I'm at Stanley's house. I was searching the greenhouse and I found a long, wavy, light brown hair. The root appears to be intact. I watch CSI. That means we have DNA, right?"

"Yeah, but we'd have to have someone in custody to match the DNA, and even if we get a match it only proves he was in the greenhouse and probably took the orchid. Doesn't prove he's the killer."

"Oh, come on. It's too much of a coincidence. I'm sure this hair belongs to the crazy-eyed VW van guy. He was there when Stanley was shot!"

"So was Archer."

"You know, you can be a real buzzkill. I have to stay with Brooke. Can you come pick this up after you transport the safe?"

"I guess I can do that. How long are you going to be at Godard's house?"

"I don't know. Call me on my cell before you leave."

When we disconnected I felt let-down. I'd expected Faulkner to be excited about my discovery. Buddy and I went inside and I presented the bagged hair to Brooke and Robbyn, who were *much* more appreciative. They watched CSI too.

"What I don't understand," said Robbyn, "is why an entire crew of trained crime scene investigators didn't find that hair."

Good question. I thought about it for a moment. "Maybe it wasn't there on Sunday. Maybe the orchid thief came back looking for the journal." I felt a chill as I said the words, instinctively knowing they were true, remembering Buddy's raised hackles as he sniffed around the greenhouse door.

I dashed into the kitchen and threw the deadbolt on the back door again.

The only room that remained to be searched was the kitchen. I didn't expect to find anything there, but I went through the motions anyway. I opened the refrigerator and bagged up anything that would spoil, leaving the contents of the freezer in place after examining them. I dug through all the cabinets and drawers and looked under the table and chairs. I even opened the curtains to make sure nothing had been concealed behind them.

When I returned to the living room Brooke and Robbyn had collapsed on the couch with Buddy between them.

"Had enough for today?" I asked.

"Absolutely," said Robbyn. "I'm ready for a cocktail."

"I'll follow you back to the condo," I said, handing Brooke the bag of groceries. "I took these out of the fridge so they wouldn't go bad."

She looked inside the bag and a tear slid down her cheek. "Thank you," she whispered.

Chapter 19

We caravanned back to Redwood Shores and Buddy and I escorted the two women up to Brooke's apartment. Once we were inside with the door locked I handed Buddy's leash to Robbyn and asked them to wait by the door while I took a quick look around. There were no culprits lurking in any of the closets, under the beds, or in the shower.

I'd missed lunch, so Brooke made me a tuna salad sandwich, which I shared with Buddy.

Robbyn blended a pitcher of margaritas and she and Brooke sipped daintily from oversized crystal martini glasses rimmed with salt.

At 3:30 Faulkner called.

"We're at Brooke's condo," I said.

"On my way."

Faulkner arrived about ten minutes later. Robbyn offered him a margarita, which he declined, and Brooke offered him coffee, which he accepted. I presented him with the bagged hair. As he studied it I told him what Brooke had said about the stolen orchid, that it would be priceless to a hybridizer, but worthless without the journal.

Faulkner asked for the journal and I said, "You can read it, but you can't keep it. I have a plan."

He cocked an eyebrow at me. "It's evidence," he said.

"Maybe."

"What's your plan?"

"I'm going to take it with me to a meeting of the Orchid Society."

I'd come up with the idea while driving back from Stanley's house. I would go to a meeting of the local chapter, make an announcement about Stanley's death and the theft of his hybrid, announce that I had his notes on the process, and show the identikit picture of the crazy-eyed guy in the van. I didn't think Faulkner needed to know all the details, but I hadn't counted on his keen deductive reasoning.

"You're going to set yourself up using the journal as bait," he said.

"Would you have a problem with that?"

"Where's the journal?"

"In my office safe." I shot a glance at Brooke. Her mouth was open, but no sound was coming out. Robbyn was smiling behind the rim of her glass.

"I'll follow you back to your office," said Faulkner.

"Can't. I have to stay with Brooke until my associate arrives."

"What time will that be?"

"Nine o'clock."

Faulkner looked from me to Brooke, and turned back to me again. "I'll pick it up in the morning."

"What if I make you a copy?" I volunteered.

"Are you always this stubborn?"

"Pretty much."

Faulkner finished his coffee, set the delicate china cup and saucer in the sink, and headed for the door. I followed.

He turned to face me before stepping outside. "I have new respect for Bill Anderson," he said, and was gone.

I let out the breath I'd been holding and bolted the door behind him.

"I think I'll have that margarita now," I said to Robbyn.

She laughed while filling a glass for me, and I took a long swallow, feeling the warmth of the tequila spread through my belly. Just what I needed.

I described my plan to the two women as we sat around the kitchen island sipping our drinks.

When I had finished, Brooke said, "That sounds really dangerous. What if the killer is at the meeting? Maybe we should go with you."

"Not a good idea," I said. "I won't be able to protect you and watch my own back at the same time."

"I was thinking *we* could watch your back."

"And what would you do if you saw this guy come up behind me?" I asked, holding up the identikit picture.

Robbyn grinned. "Swift kick to the gonads should do the trick." I looked at her. "I took a self-defense class back home," she continued. "Did some serious damage to the instructor. We'd gone out a couple of times and he was *not* a gentleman. I managed to bruise his manhood even through all that padding." She giggled and sipped her margarita.

"Okay," I said. "What about you, Brooke?"

"I work out, but I don't have any kind of training." She got up and went into the living room, returning with her purse. She reached inside, "But I have one of these," she said, taking out a small, pink stun gun.

"Huh," I said. "I may have underestimated you two. Okay, you can come with me but you have to stay in the back of the room and try to be inconspicuous. Where's your computer?" I asked Brooke.

"In the bedroom."

Brooke escorted me to a small desk facing the window in her bedroom. I logged onto Internet Explorer and did a Google search for the American Orchid Society in the San Francisco Bay area, and couldn't find a listing. I tried a search using just the word 'orchid' and got hits for branches of the Orchid Society of California in Oakland and in San Francisco. I kept reading and finally found the Peninsula Orchid Society in San Mateo. Brooke said she thought the club meetings Stanley had attended were in San Mateo, so I hoped I'd found the right group.

I dialed the number and spoke with a

woman who told me that the next meeting would be Friday night, at the San Mateo Garden Center on Parkside Way. I asked if non-members would be allowed to attend and she said that prospective members could make a small donation at the door. *Excellent.*

CHAPTER 20

WHEN THE CLEANING CREW HAD finished their work they hauled their supplies back out through Nick Lawrence's garage, loading everything into the van. The crew supervisor set the thumb lock and closed the door between the garage and the house. Once he was out in the driveway, he used a remote to close the overhead door. Nina wondered where Lawrence sequestered the children he'd purchased from Giordano when the cleaning service was in his home. Perhaps in a locked, soundproof space like a basement. That was a problem she's have to leave for the police.

Nina spent the rest of Tuesday morning and early afternoon in the garage, using her Android phone to Google her remaining targets. When Lawrence had been dispatched, only seven would remain from Fredo Giordano's client list. She'd considered long and hard what she would do once every name on that list had been checked off. Maybe take a tropical vacation, or begin a new list using the Megan's Law website. Nina knew she'd never abandon her mission. She was driven by the need to annihilate anyone who tortured innocent children the way she had been tortured by her own father. She couldn't and wouldn't stop... unless someone stopped her.

At 5:15 she heard Lawrence's car in the driveway just before the automatic door began to rise. Nina remained in her hiding place until he had parked the car, turned off the engine, and lowered the overhead door. Then she slowly rose to a standing position behind the storage boxes which had hidden her from view. The only illumination in the garage was the light box on the automatic door mechanism housed on the ceiling. Nina wore dark clothes, and she was halfway across the room before Lawrence even noticed her.

His mouth opened in surprise as Nina hit him with the taser. She removed her new stiletto switchblade from her pocket and waited for his twitching to stop, then slid the razor-sharp knife into his solar plexus and, in a practiced motion, angled it upward into his heart.

After retracting the blade, she wrapped

the knife in a scarf she'd brought along, tucked it back into her pocket, and removed her latex gloves. Not having fingerprints was an advantage, but she didn't want blood on her hands, and her scarred fingertips could potentially be used to link her to a crime scene if she was ever caught. Donning a clean pair of gloves, she approached the wall-mounted garage door control panel, and was about to press the button when she realized Lawrence's body would be visible from the street. She found a folded tarp on a workbench and draped it over the body, making sure he was thoroughly covered, then pressed the button to open the overhead door. She waited until it was open, then hit the switch to close it again.

Moving quickly, Nina dashed under the closing door, but as she passed through the opening the door suddenly came to a stop. Her body had tripped the automatic sensor which kept the door from closing. Nina decided to keep going rather than risk drawing attention to herself, or to the repeatedly opening and closing garage door. She moved casually down the street to her rental car and breathed a sigh of relief when no vehicles passed her as she drove away.

Seven to go, she thought with satisfaction as she made the short drive back to her hotel.

Chapter 21

Jim called at 8:58 to tell me he was in the parking lot. I picked up the identikit drawing and asked Brooke if I could borrow it until tomorrow.

She said, "Of course," and took another sip of her third margarita.

I hooked Buddy to his leash and slung my bag over my shoulder.

Once I was outside and heard the deadbolt latch behind me, I dug the journal out of my purse and unzipped my fanny pack holster. I walked down the steps listening intently for any sound, watching Buddy for a startle response. When I reached the parking lot I spotted Jim's Honda, but I didn't acknowledge him, in case someone was watching.

I drove to the marina keeping an eye

on my rearview mirror. It was dark, but the streets were lit well enough for me to see make, model, and color of the other cars on the road. I didn't spot a VW van.

When we arrived home I walked Buddy around the marina grounds before unlocking the office. I poured him a bowl of kibble and freshened the water in his dish, then booted up the computer and checked my e-mail. I had a response from the International Orchid Show people with a short list of the members who had pre-registered to exhibit new hybrids. They had given me names and identified the chapter each belonged to, but there was no personal contact information. Brad Tomlinson and Beth Kilburn belonged to the San Francisco affiliate. Stanley Godard and Bernard Cross were members of the Peninsula Orchid Society. *Bingo.* Maybe I'd get a chance to meet Cross on Friday night.

I Googled the three names and found articles published by Tomlinson and Kilburn, but nothing about Cross whatsoever. I checked the online white pages and got addresses and phone numbers for Tomlinson and Kilburn, but again nothing for Cross. If Cross was the guy I was looking for maybe he lived in his van.

I printed Tomlinson and Kilburn's

contact data, then took out Stanley's orchid journal and photocopied every page. This took a while. When I was done I made twenty copies of the identikit picture. I checked my watch. It was almost 11:00. I wondered if Bill was down on the boat. Probably not. I hadn't seen his Mustang in the lot when we arrived, and Buddy would have reacted if he'd arrived after we did. When Buddy hears Bill's car approaching he goes a little crazy. Of course, Bill could be driving one of the department's unmarked cars. He does that when he expects to be called to a crime scene, even if he's off-duty, because his own fire engine red Mustang is too recognizable.

I locked the journal copy in my safe and tucked the original back in my purse, then Buddy and I locked up the office and walked down to the boat.

The Cheoy Lee was empty and dark when we climbed aboard, and I went from room to room turning on lights. It was too late to call Elizabeth, so I made myself a chicken salad and turned on the news.

At 11:45 Bill came in looking haggard. I took two bottles of Guinness out of the fridge and popped them open, handing one to him.

"Tough day?"

"This whole Nina Jezek thing is a can of worms. Another body was found today, on Mohican Way, garlic in the wound. His name was Edward Mitchell. A personal injury attorney, also with ties to Giordano."

"Is internal affairs getting involved again?"

Nina had been a swing shift data entry clerk for the RCPD before it was discovered she was a homicidal maniac.

"Naturally," he said, and downed half his Stout.

"Kind of muddies the water, doesn't it?"

He silently drank the remainder of his beer, and nodded.

"So apparently Nina is targeting people who did business with Giordano. Is there any way to get a list of his clients?"

"We've put in a request to the FBI VCAC unit, but there's no telling how long they'll take to respond." He sighed.

"Nothing you can do about that," I said.

"Nope."

"So, let's go to bed."

I figured sex would take his mind off his troubles, and I was right. Thirty minutes later Bill was sleeping soundly and I was wide awake, going over Brooke's case in my mind. I needed to question Archer without

Faulkner interfering, but when would I have the time to do that if I spent my days guarding Brooke? Maybe Jim could spare one of his agents to babysit Brooke for a few hours. But even if I had the time, how would I get in to see Archer? The research firm was like Fort Knox. If I had his home address I could corner him there, or I could arrive early at his office and wait for him to show up. That seemed like the best idea.

Once I had Archer cornered, the problem would be convincing him to talk to me. I didn't have anything to threaten him with, but he didn't know that. I could tell him that Stanley kept a journal, which was true. Maybe I'd even show him the one that was in my purse and imply that there was something in it about him. That might work.

I finally drifted off, only to be assaulted by dreams about Nina Jezek, who appeared in my subconscious alternately as a crazed killer and as an innocent child who had been abused.

CHAPTER 22

AFTER DISPATCHING NICK LAWRENCE ON Tuesday afternoon Nina had immediately moved on to the next man on Giordano's client list. Edward Mitchell was a personal injury lawyer with an office on Woodside Road in Redwood City. His previous purchases from Giordano showed that he favored boys between the ages of five and eight. He'd made seven purchases in the last nine years, the most recent being almost a year ago. Nina knew it was unlikely that little boy had survived his encounter with Mitchell. These well-to-do pedophiles could not afford to be identified, should their victims ever seek help from the authorities.

She parked her rental car in the lot adjacent to Mitchell's office, noting the lights in the suite were still on, and smiled to herself.

She kept her eyes on the front door while removing the switchblade from the scarf in her pocket. Pulling a packet of wet wipes from her shoulder bag, she meticulously cleaned the weapon, then applied a fresh coat of garlic extract to the blade.

Just as she was finishing her preparations, the door to Mitchell's office opened and a man stepped outside, locking the door behind him. Nina checked the DMV photo of her target. Five-foot-nine, a hundred and eighty soft pounds, dark hair, and a goatee. With any luck at all she'd finish Mitchell off tonight, get a good night's sleep, and move on to the final six tomorrow.

Mitchell drove a black Range Rover Evoque with tinted windows. He used a remote to unlock and start the SUV, lit a cigar, and climbed into the driver's seat. Nina followed as he exited the lot onto Woodside Road, her nondescript rental car making her all but invisible. Mitchell drove a few blocks and pulled into a restaurant parking lot. Nina had been to this restaurant before. In fact it was where she'd first made contact with Giordano, Mitchell's supplier. She wondered if someone had taken Giordano's place and was meeting Mitchell in order to sell him another innocent victim.

Nina parked an aisle away from Mitchell and followed him into the restaurant, waiting patiently as the hostess seated him at a window table. When the hostess returned, Nina told her she didn't have a reservation, but pointed to a vacant table near Mitchell. The hostess glanced at the reservations book, nodded, and picked up a menu.

"Will you be dining alone tonight?"

"Unless I get lucky," Nina said, with a wink.

The hostess blushed at Nina's bold comment and led her to the table, handed her the menu, and returned to the podium. A busboy was filling a water goblet at Mitchell's table while he read over the menu. Nina glanced at her own menu only long enough to determine that they served a Chef's Salad. She continued to hold the menu, and watched Mitchell as he ordered his entrée.

Mitchell took his time over dinner, and no one approached him other than the serving staff. When he ordered coffee, Nina motioned to the waiter and requested her check. She was in her car waiting when Mitchell came outside. Nina knew he lived on Mohican Way in Redwood City, but followed him nevertheless, in case he made another stop along the way.

Mitchell drove directly to his luxury home,

parked in the three-car garage, and closed the overhead door. Nina waited on the street as a few rooms in the house were illuminated. Six floor-to-ceiling windows faced a wraparound deck. After only a few minutes Mitchell came out onto the deck holding a rocks glass and talking on his cell phone.

Nina stood in the shadows, watching, until he returned to the house leaving the French doors open behind him. She silently climbed the outer steps to the deck, taser in one hand, stiletto in the other.

When Mitchell finished his call he refilled his glass and turned back toward the open doors. A gasp caught in his throat as Nina hit him with the taser. The rocks glass shattered on the tile floor and Mitchell collapsed at Nina's feet. She dispatched him promptly, and made a point of turning off the lights before leaving.

Six to go.

CHAPTER 23

WHEN MY BEDSIDE DREAM MACHINE went off I lunged blindly for the snooze button. The next thing I knew Bill was standing by the bed, fully dressed, with a cup of coffee in his hand. He looked great, but it was the coffee that got my attention. He set the cup on the nightstand and said, "I have to go. Buddy's already had his breakfast and a walk."

I struggled into a sitting position and tried to focus my eyes on the clock. "What time is it?"

"Seven fifteen."

"Oh *crap*!" If I was going to catch Archer before work I'd have to skip my workout, again. I kissed Bill before he went out the door, grabbed the coffee, and took it with me into the shower.

Buddy and I were on the road by 7:30. I called Jim on his cell and asked him to keep an eye on Brooke until I got there, telling him briefly what I planned to do. When I ended the call I turned off my cell and tossed it into my purse.

At 7:45 Buddy and I were parked in the research firm lot next to Archer's assigned parking space. I hadn't noticed it when Faulkner and I were here before because the Benz was in the space, but there was a red 'CFO' painted on the macadam.

My hair was wet and I didn't have any make-up on, which made me feel defenseless. My mini cassette recorder was in the pocket of my shorts, set on voice activate. That made me feel only slightly more empowered.

I hunted through my purse for lip-gloss as I watched employees arrive for work. When I found the lip-gloss I slathered some on, then started searching for mascara. I was putting on a second coat when Archer's Mercedes pulled into the lot. As he parked in his spot I grabbed the journal, bolted out of my car, and hopped into Archer's passenger seat. The look on his face was one of stunned disbelief.

"Before you say anything," I held up my hand like a stop sign, "you should know that

I found Stanley Godard's journal." I showed him the leather bound notebook. "I haven't taken it to the police yet because I wanted to give you a chance to explain yourself first."

"I told that detective everything," Archer sputtered.

"I don't think so. You said you had invoice and check copies in the suitcase you brought into Stanley's office. That implies that the original invoices and checks actually exist."

Archer's mouth opened and closed a couple of times and he reflexively loosened the knot in his tie. I decided to wait him out.

After a minute he shook his head and mumbled, "I can't go to jail."

Excellent, I thought. "That's not up to me," I said, imagining Archer with a trophy wife who would soon have to learn to clip coupons. "You can tell me what happened or you can talk to Detective Faulkner. Your choice."

"You wouldn't understand," he sighed.

"Let's find out," I said, waiting for his story to begin.

"Erika is my third wife," he said, not making eye contact with me as he spoke. "I still pay the other two alimony, and Erika is very demanding. I had to do *something*."

Sometimes my powers of deduction amaze even me.

"So?" I said.

"So I set up a dummy corporation using a P.O. Box."

"And you submitted fraudulent invoices."

"Yes," he whispered. "When this comes out I'll be ruined."

I ignored his anxiety and asked the question that had been haunting me. "Why did you choose Stanley Godard to do the audit?"

"Because he worked alone. I didn't think he'd be so thorough."

"And when he found out what you were doing, you had to keep him quiet." I hoped the recorder was picking all of this up. It wouldn't be admissible in court, but it would give Faulkner something to work with.

"Yes," Archer murmured.

I waited. When he said nothing further, I prodded, "And?"

Archer looked at me forlornly. "I didn't have much left in the bank, so I submitted more invoices."

"For how much?"

"Another hundred thousand. As soon as I got the money I called Godard for an appointment. I said I'd found the documents he was looking for."

"Did you offer him the whole hundred thousand?"

"Fifty."

"What did he say?"

"He was outraged, almost apoplectic. Then someone knocked on the back door and he went to answer it."

This wasn't what I wanted to hear. Archer was attempting to direct me back toward an unknown subject.

"Then what happened?" I said.

"I heard the shot. I was so terrified that I left the suitcase full of money on his desk and ran."

"Did you see who fired the shot?"

"I really didn't. I just ran out the front door."

"I don't believe you," I said. "I think you killed Stanley to keep him quiet, or hired someone to do it for you."

Archer mutely shook his head, then his eyes locked on mine. "I have fifty thousand left. It's yours if you'll give me that journal."

I got out of the Benz and returned to my car, where Buddy was waiting. I locked the doors, rolled up the windows, and cranked the engine.

Archer was out of his car, waving his arms frantically, shouting, "Please! Please!"

I almost ran over him trying to get out of the parking space. Buddy started barking and Archer fell silent as I pulled away.

I called Faulkner on my way to Brooke's condo.

"Where the hell are you?" he said. "I've been calling you since eight!"

"Sorry. I overslept. I'm on my way to Brooke's. Can I give you the journal copy tomorrow?"

"You're a pain in the ass, Hunter."

"Yeah, I know."

We disconnected and I called Jim. "I'm on my way," I said.

"Get anything out of Archer?"

"Yes, but not what I wanted. He admitted to the embezzling, but insists he didn't kill Stanley or hire someone else to do it."

"Do you believe him?"

"I don't know. Maybe. Have you spotted anyone suspicious lurking around Brooke's condo?"

"Nope."

When I arrived at the Redwood Shores complex I gave Jim a copy of the identikit sketch and asked him to be at the San Mateo Garden Center at 9:00 tomorrow night, telling him about my plan for the evening. I hooked Buddy's leash to his collar, collected my shoulder bag, and locked up the car.

I dialed Brooke on my cell as we climbed the stairs. "I'm here," I said.

Robbyn opened the door when I knocked, and made a fuss over Buddy while I secured the deadbolt.

I returned the original identikit picture to Brooke, poured myself a cup of coffee, and sat down at the kitchen island.

"What's on the agenda for today?" I asked.

"I'm trying to decide what kind of flowers to order for Stanley's funeral," Brooke said. "I was originally thinking orchids, but the blooms only last a couple of weeks once they're cut, and they last up to two months on a live plant. I hate to think of all those orchid plants losing their blooms. I could have the florist send enough live orchids to fill the chapel, but then what would I do with them afterwards? I already have a greenhouse full of orchids to take care of, and I don't even know what they need. I can't sell them. They were Stanley's pride and joy. I guess I'm feeling a little overwhelmed."

"You could probably take a class on how to care for the orchids," I offered. "And I'm sure there's a lot of information available online. Tomorrow night, when we're at the orchid club meeting, we can ask around and see if there's somebody local who would be knowledgeable enough to tutor you."

Brooke's face brightened. "That's a wonderful idea. Honestly, Nikki, I don't know what I'd do without you." And she dissolved into tears.

Robbyn put her arms around Brooke's shoulders and I fetched the box of Kleenex. When the sobbing subsided I asked the location and time of the funeral service on Saturday. I went into Brooke's bedroom, turned on her laptop, did a Google search, and started calling florists. The third one I called agreed to rent us a dozen large, potted orchid plants, which they would retrieve after the service. Problem solved.

I hung up the phone and Brooke threw her arms around me and started sobbing all over again. I gently patted her back, resisting the urge to pull away.

When Brooke's tears had dried, she told me that Stanley's family was flying in for the service on Saturday morning: both parents, a brother, and a sister. They would be staying at the Airport Hilton.

"Do you think I should take them out to dinner after the funeral?" she asked.

"Why don't you wait and see how you feel," I suggested.

"You're right, of course. It's just that Stanley's childhood is such a mystery to me."

"How long will they be in town?"

"Just overnight. They're leaving on Sunday."

"That does limit your window of opportunity."

Brooke needed groceries, so we all piled into my BMW and drove to Whole Foods on Hillsdale Boulevard. Robbyn sat in the back seat with Buddy and was subjected to a thorough face washing.

I parked in the cool underground lot, cracked the windows, and locked the doors, telling Buddy we'd be back pretty soon.

It took Brooke almost an hour to fill her cart because she hadn't made a shopping list and had to go up and down every aisle. I wondered if she and Stanley had ever gone shopping together. She was driving me crazy, and I didn't even have OCD.

There were a few long-haired and bearded men in the store, but none of them matched the identikit sketch.

As we rode down in the elevator I felt a prickly sensation on the back of my neck. It's a feeling I've learned not to ignore. I threw my shoulder bag into the cart and pushed Brooke and Robbyn to the back of the elevator.

"Get down," I said.

I kept the cart in front of me and unholstered the Ruger. The ride down to the garage took only seconds, but it seemed like hours before the doors slid open revealing the deserted basement vestibule. I could hear Buddy's bark echoing throughout the underground garage.

"Stay here," I said to Brooke and Robbyn.

I crouched low, hoping to make less of a target, holding the Ruger double-handed and aiming at the ground in front of me for safety's sake. I quickly checked the stairs to see if anyone was lurking there before stepping through the glass doors into the garage.

Buddy was still sounding off as I approached the car, revolving slowly as I walked, trying to look in all directions at once. I heard a car engine rumble to life and turned quickly to my right as an old orange VW van rattled toward the exit. I holstered the gun and took off running. I needed to catch up with that van and at least get the license plate number, but the garage was dimly lit and the van was already twenty yards away. I kept running until I hit the street, but by then the van was nowhere in sight. *Crap!*

When I got back to the car Brooke and Robbyn had used my keys to unlock the trunk and were unloading groceries from the cart.

"I told you to stay in the elevator," I said.

"But you didn't tell us why," said Robbyn.

"I didn't *know* why," I snapped.

I took a minute to survey the outside of my BMW. Someone had used a crowbar to try and wrench open the passenger side door. "Shit," I said. "Give me my keys."

Robbyn tossed the keys to me and I unlocked the car, hooked Buddy to his leash, and let him out. I tried to calm him down, but his whole body was vibrating and his hackles were still up.

"It was the guy in the van," I said. "He tried to break into my car. Must be pretty desperate if he was willing to face Buddy."

It suddenly occurred to me that if the van guy was the killer, he had a gun. My knees buckled as I realized what might have happened to Buddy if he had gotten the car door open. I sat down hard on the pavement and hugged my dog, heart pounding in my chest. Buddy normally likes hugs, but he struggled away from me and started off toward where the van had been parked. I grabbed the leash and he dragged me a few feet.

"Buddy, stay," I said.

He turned to look at me, furrowed his brow, and whimpered. He wanted to follow the scent.

"He's gone," I said. "Get back in the car, please."

Brooke and Robbyn had returned the cart to the vestibule and were standing off to the side of the car, staring at me.

Finally Brooke spoke. "How did you know he was here?"

I got Buddy into the backseat and turned to face them. "I didn't," I said. "I just had a bad feeling, and then I heard Buddy barking."

Robbyn tilted her head to the side. "So, you're a PI and a psychic?"

"Nothing like that," I said. "I just get feelings sometimes, and I've learned to pay attention to them."

We all climbed into the car, and I made sure the doors were locked and the windows rolled up before we took off.

Driving back to Redwood Shores I thought about the timing of the attempted break-in. It seemed significant to me that the first time the crazy-eyed van guy came after the journal was the same day I confronted Archer. I replayed the conversation in my head, thinking through the process he had used to embezzle.

I don't know much about accounting, but when I was working security for a department store chain, part of my job was to keep an eye on the flow of money going out of the store, and I knew that all invoices had to be signed off on by the purchasing manager. What if Archer had a partner within the research firm? What if the guy in the van worked in the purchasing department? Of course, that wouldn't explain the theft of the orchid, but it might explain why no one had come after the journal until now.

Chapter 24

When we arrived at Brooke's condo I escorted the two women upstairs and, after a quick search of the apartment, left them with Buddy while I made three trips to and from the car lugging bags of groceries.

Once we were all safely locked inside I called Faulkner and recapped my conversation with Archer that morning and the attempted break-in at the Whole Foods parking garage. He was not happy.

"Stay away from Archer," he said. "You may have compromised any case we have against him."

"Don't you even want to hear the tape? He confessed to embezzling from his employer!"

"He confessed to *you*."

"It's on *tape*!"

"It's *inadmissible*. I believe he's been skimming from his employer, but I don't think he's a killer. I guess I might as well check out the recording, though. I'll meet you at your office tomorrow at eight. And I want that damn journal."

"You can't have the journal yet. But I made you a copy."

"I could charge you with obstruction, you know."

"Yeah, but you're not going to do that. Besides, I only need it for a few more days. I'm going to a meeting of Stanley's orchid club tomorrow night. Hey, you want to come?"

"That's not a bad idea."

I gave Faulkner the address and directions, and told him I'd meet him there at 7:45. I didn't mention that Brooke and Robbyn were coming and that I was counting on him to protect Brooke while I spoke to the club members.

I was about to hang up when I remembered something else Archer had said.

"Archer said he had fifty thousand dollars in the suitcase he took into Stanley's office."

"So?"

"Did the forensics team find that

much burned money in the remains of Stanley's office?"

"There were some charred bills recovered, but I don't think it could have been that much."

So maybe Archer had lied to me about how much money he'd left behind, but why would he do that unless he was hiding something else?

Brooke, Robbyn, and I spent the rest of the day going over the details for Stanley's funeral. As Brooke suspected, he had planned the whole affair in advance. It was sad to think that Stanley didn't even trust the details of his own passing to someone else, and remarkable to realize he'd trusted Brooke enough to commit to spending the rest of his life with her. He must have been over-the-moon in love with her.

Jim called my cell from the parking lot of Brooke's complex at 8:45, saying he was ready to take over. I thanked him again, relayed the events of the day, and told him I'd be flaunting the journal on the way to my car yet again, hoping to draw attention away from Brooke.

I bid the ladies good night and made sure they had Jim's cell number before exiting the condo with Buddy. As I waited for the sound of the deadbolt, I looked up J.V. Trusty's home number on my smartphone. Buddy and I made our way down the stairs and I pocketed the phone so I'd have one hand free for the leash and the journal, and the other free for the gun in my fanny pack holster.

I ignored Jim's car as we strolled to my Bimmer, holding the journal in my left hand, the loop from Buddy's leash around my wrist. We got to the car without being approached by any crazy-eyed van drivers, but the lot was dark, and he could easily have been out there somewhere, watching.

Once we were locked in the car I pulled the cell from my pocket, pushed the send button to dial J.V., and set the phone on speaker mode.

"Trusty and Associates," J.V. answered.

"Hey, J.V. It's Nikki."

"*Hello*, Nicoli! How *are* you? And how's Buddy?"

"We're both fine. How are you and Scott doing?"

"Better every day. Thank you for asking. So, what's going on?"

"What? I can't call just to check in on two of my favorite people?"

"Of course you can. Now spill it."

I laughed. Being a PI, naturally J.V. had developed a sixth sense about when something was amiss.

"It's Nina. She's back in the States, and she's killed two more men, that we know of."

"Holy shit! I thought she was overseas."

"She was, but not anymore. I'm involved in a case right now that's taking up my days, and I have my regular clients to see to at night, but when I get this day-job resolved I was wondering if you and Scott would like me to try and track her down, and put an end to her rampage."

J.V. was silent for a long moment, and I wondered if I'd lost the connection.

"Are you still there?"

"I'm here. I was just thinking. You've already done what Scott hired you to do. You identified his mother's killer and, to some extent, determined why she chose to do away with his mom. I don't want you to put yourself in danger, Nicoli. The police can take it from here. They have more resources than you do."

"I appreciate that, J.V., I really do. Maybe you should check with Scott in the morning and see if he agrees with that decision. You're right that the police have more resources than I do, but I'm more flexible than they are, if you know what I mean."

"I know exactly what you mean. They never would have caught her in the act the way you did. But that doesn't mean you should risk your life trying to stop her."

"Yeah, I know. Call me after you talk to Scott."

"I'll do that. Thank you for letting me know that she's back."

We ended the call and I focused on driving for the remaining few minutes it took to get to the marina.

Chapter 25

Buddy and I strolled around the grounds before going to the office. Once again I hadn't seen Bill's Mustang in the lot, but I never knew when he might be driving an unmarked car. I fed Buddy and gave him fresh water, then called Bill's cell.

"Anderson."

"Hunter."

"Hey babe, where are you?"

"We're in the office. Just got back from Brooke's. Where are you?"

"I'm onboard your boat. Are you coming down any time soon?"

"I need to work tonight. I was hoping you could spend the evening with Buddy again."

"Sure. I can do that."

My next call was to Elizabeth. I'd spotted

her VW Beetle in the owner's lot, so I knew she was home.

She answered on the second ring. "Hi honey. What are you up to?"

"I need to do a dinner survey at Michelino's in San Mateo, and I was hoping you'd come along. I know you have to work tomorrow, but I could really use a sounding board."

"Sure. As long as you don't keep me out too late. When are you picking me up?"

"Fifteen minutes. I just need to get Buddy down to the boat and change clothes."

"See you then."

I hooked Buddy's leash to his collar, locked up the office, and trotted toward the gate.

Once Bill and Buddy were settled in the pilot house watching the news, I stripped off my shorts, shirt, and shoes, and slipped into a black halter dress and a pair of peep-toe pumps. I scrunched some gel into my curls, swiped on some red lip gloss, and touched up my mascara, then transferred everything from my shoulder bag and fanny pack holster to my black pistol purse.

Giving Bill a quick kiss and Buddy an ear scratch, I said, "Thank you for watching the pup," and scrambled up the companionway.

Elizabeth was waiting on her dock steps when I arrived at her trawler.

"You look fabulous," she said, and took my arm as we strode up the ramp to shore.

Once we were in my Bimmer on our way to San Mateo she turned to me and asked, "What's happening with the murder investigation?"

"Well, I have two suspects. There's the crazy-eyed guy who drives a rattletrap VW van, and there's a guy named Archer who hired Stanley to handle an audit for his company. I think Stanley caught him embezzling."

"Tell me everything."

In the fifteen minutes it took us to reach 25th Avenue in San Mateo, I managed to fill Elizabeth in on all of the details of Stanley's case to date.

"So, what do you think?" I asked.

"I like Archer for it. You might be right about the van driver stealing Stanley's orchid, but that doesn't make him a killer. Just a thief."

"Then why was he at Stanley's office when he was shot?"

"Maybe he wanted to make sure Stanley was *at* his office before he went to his house to steal the orchid. I think Archer has more to lose. He lied to you about how much money he left in Stanley's office, right? Faulkner said there wasn't enough charred cash to amount to fifty thousand. So I think we can assume that Archer was lying about what happened to Stanley too."

"Yeah. I was thinking the same thing."

We locked up the car and approached the restaurant.

"Anything special the owner wants you to watch for tonight? Are you counting Al's drinks again?"

The last time Elizabeth had been to Michelino's with me I'd been tasked with counting the number of drinks one of the bartenders had during his shift. The owner wasn't concerned about a few drinks, but in the ninety minutes I'd been there I'd watched Al prepare and consume five screwdrivers. The man was Italian and had amazing alcohol tolerance. He was still functioning fully when I left for home.

"Not tonight. There's a new server I'm supposed to check out. After I caught Martina till tapping I suggested running background checks before hiring new servers, but the owner prefers to trust his own instincts. I shouldn't complain. It's that kind of thinking that keeps me in business."

The new server's name was Dominic, and his area of the restaurant was up front by the windows. Not knowing when I'd get there, I hadn't bothered to make a reservation, and no tables were available in Dominic's area at the moment. I told the maître d' we'd wait in the bar until something opened up.

Al was on duty. He smiled at me as we perched on stools at his end of the bar. Al is in his sixties and has a full head of wavy white hair and a lazy, Dean Martin smile. Last time he'd served me he had asked if I was single because he had two sons he wanted to introduce me to. I'd found him charming, and he was an excellent bartender, in spite of his drinking habit.

Al placed napkins on the bar in front of us and asked what we'd like to drink. I ordered a bottle of Perrier and Elizabeth requested a tall mudslide. Al gave her a wink and immediately served my water in a glass filled with ice and a wedge of lime, then set about preparing the mudslide. His hands were skilled and his movements almost elegant as he mixed the ingredients in an old fashioned cocktail shaker. After pouring the chocolaty concoction into a tall glass he carefully added some shaved dark chocolate to the top and offered it to Elizabeth along with a wrapped straw.

"Enjoy," he said, and moved down the bar to take care of another customer.

Elizabeth took a sip. "Wow!" she exclaimed. "That guy is an artist! This is the best mudslide I've ever tasted."

"When he comes back you should tell him that."

"I definitely will. So what else is going on in your life?"

"Well, Nina's back."

Elizabeth choked on a swallow of her drink and I slapped her on the back until she could breathe normally again.

"Next time you have news like that, please wait until I'm done swallowing!"

"Sorry. You asked."

"When did she get back, and how do you *know* she's back?"

"Actually, I don't know for sure that it's her, but Bill caught two cases this week where men were killed with a long, double-edged knife coated with garlic."

"That sounds like Nina all right. Two in one week? She's been busy. Who were the victims?"

"A guy named Nick Lawrence was found on Wednesday morning in his garage. He lived in Westport. The second victim was Edward Mitchell. He was a personal injury attorney who lived on Mohican Way. The only thing they had in common was an association with Alfredo Giordano."

"Wait. I know that name."

"He was another one of Nina's victims. She killed him last December. He's the guy who lived up in Woodside Hills. You and Jack followed Nina home from his house the morning after she killed him."

"Oh yeah. Good times." She smirked and drank some more of her mudslide.

The maître d' chose that moment to approach and informed us that a window table had become available. Al returned from serving other patrons and asked if we'd like our drinks added to our dinner tab.

"Yes, thank you, Al," I said.

He handed a drink slip to the maître d', and as he withdrew his hand Elizabeth touched his wrist and said, "You make an amazing mudslide, Al. Best I've ever tasted."

Al beamed at the praise, raised Elizabeth's hand, and kissed it. "It was my pleasure," he crooned.

I would enjoy adding these little flourishes to my report. The owner hadn't requested a bar survey, but I'd toss it in for free, giving Al his much deserved props.

The maître d' carried our drinks to the dining room on a tray, placed them on the table, and pulled out our chairs for us, waiting until we were seated before placing cloth napkins on our laps. He informed us that our server would be Dominic, bowed slightly, and departed.

Dominic approached the table immediately. Handing each of us a menu, he introduced himself and asked if we'd like to hear tonight's specials. He was in his late twenties, dark haired, clean shaven, and quite handsome.

Elizabeth smiled and said, "I'd *love* to hear the specials, Dominic."

Her suggestive tone caught him off guard and he blushed, cleared his throat, and proceeded to recite the entrées the chef recommended tonight.

Elizabeth listened with rapt attention until he was done and I asked if we could have a few minutes with the menu.

"Very good," he commented, and left to tend to his other tables.

"You," I said, "are an outrageous flirt."

"I know. So what are you going to do about Nina?"

"Maybe nothing. I called J.V. and he suggested I stay out of it. I asked him to speak with Scott about the situation and let me know if he agreed. According to J.V., I've already done what Scott originally hired me to do, and he doesn't want me to take any unnecessary risks where Nina is concerned."

"He's right. You have enough on your plate with Stanley's murder, and Nina is unpredictable. You need to stay safe."

"All killers are unpredictable, and safety is an illusion."

"That may be true, but it's *nice* illusion."

We considered the menu options and when Dominic returned I requested the Mushroom Asiago Chicken entrée and a house salad, and Elizabeth opted for the Garlic, Mozzarella, and Pesto Stuffed Pork Chops with the Caesar Salad. Dominic collected our menus, offered Elizabeth a shy smile, and went to place our orders.

"Yummy," Elizabeth murmured.

"Aren't you getting married sometime next year?"

She laughed out loud at my comment, and a few heads turned to see what was so funny.

"Nikki, honey, as much as I love Jack

McGuire, I will never stop appreciating beautiful men."

"Whatever."

Dominic returned shortly and served our salads. The greens were fresh, and my house dressing, creamy Italian, of course, was delicious. Two minutes after setting the salad plates on the table, he returned to ask if everything was to our satisfaction. This is one of the things I time, and Dominic was doing a first-rate job so far.

When we'd almost finished our salads, he served our entrées. My Mushroom Asiago Chicken was the perfect combination of tender chicken breasts, butter, mushrooms, garlic, white wine, heavy cream, and Asiago cheese. Each bite literally melted in my mouth. Elizabeth moaned as she chewed the first taste of her stuffed pork chops.

We enjoyed our meal and each other's company enormously. When Dominic offered dessert, Elizabeth checked her watch and said, "Another time. I'm about to turn into a pumpkin."

Dominic left our table and went behind the bar where all the servers record their orders. He returned with a black leather folder containing a cash register receipt, bowed, said, "Thank you very much, ladies," and departed.

I read over the receipt and noted that it included our drinks from the bar and the correct entrées and salads, for the correct amounts. I placed a stack of cash in the folder and pocketed the receipt.

Driving back to the marina Elizabeth chattered about a wedding dress she'd seen in Modern Bride magazine.

"It's a high-necked beaded halter, off-white of course, but the fabric covering the cleavage region is chiffon so it's translucent. Some Italian guy designed it. Wait till you see it. *So* gorgeous!"

I couldn't help laughing at her enthusiasm about a dress she'd wear only once. Of course, she and Jack might end up being one of those couples who renew their vows annually, but knowing Elizabeth she'd want a new dress every year.

I walked Elizabeth to the locked gate, then opened the office just long enough to drop off my notes and receipt for the dinner. I'd type the report tomorrow. Right now, I just wanted some Buddy and Bill time.

CHAPTER 26

ON FRIDAY MORNING I HIT the gym early and worked both my upper and lower body to make up for missed workouts. I got home in time to have breakfast with Bill and Buddy, and still made it to the office by 8:00 for my meeting with Faulkner.

Once again he asked me for the journal and, once again, I told him he couldn't have it yet. He just glared at me.

"Take the copy," I said. "You can look it over and, if you still want the original, I'll trade you for the copy in a few days. You're coming to the Orchid Club meeting tonight, right?" I took the journal copy out of the safe and gave it to him.

"I wouldn't miss it."

Buddy and I followed Faulkner outside and we walked together to the parking lot. Before getting into his Chevy P.O.S. he turned to me with a quizzical look in his eyes. "When you cornered Archer yesterday morning, you said he told you he'd embezzled the money so he could afford his trophy wife, correct?"

"Yeah. Why?"

"I checked. Archer doesn't have a wife. In fact, he's never been married. I thought you'd want to know."

What the fuck?

"Why would he lie about something like that?" I asked. "That was a pretty elaborate excuse. Not only did he tell me he was married, he said he was paying alimony to two *ex*-wives."

"No idea. See you tonight."

Faulkner started his car as I loaded Buddy into my BMW. At the last minute I remembered the tape. I jogged back to the Chevy before Faulkner pulled away. He rolled down his window and I took the tiny cassette out of my purse.

"Do you have a mini cassette player?" I asked, handing him the tape.

He raised an eyebrow. "I think I can dig one up."

I arrived at Brooke's condo complex at 8:40 and sent Jim home.

Brooke and Robbyn spent the morning going over more tedious funeral details. Brooke had somehow gotten a copy of Stanley's client list from Faulkner and had called everyone to let them know about the service.

"What about his friends?" I asked.

Brooke's lower lip trembled, "Stanley didn't have any friends. Only me."

I was afraid the water works were about to begin again, but she pulled herself together.

"Detective Faulkner is coming to the meeting tonight," I said.

"Fabulous," said Robbyn. "He is such a hottie, especially for a cop."

"You think?" I said. Faulkner was good looking and intelligent, but I wouldn't have classified him as a hottie. I looked over at Brooke and noticed that she was blushing. "What do *you* think?" I asked her.

She looked trapped, but Robbyn came to her rescue. "She's in mourning," she said. "But she likes him… a lot."

"Really?"

"Totally," said Robbyn. "But she believes it would be inappropriate to start dating anyone so soon after Stanley's death."

"Stop talking about me as if I weren't here," said Brooke.

"Have you ever gone out with a cop?" I asked.

"No."

"Have you?" asked Robbyn.

"I've been dating an RCPD Detective for the last seven months," I said.

They both stared at me with their mouths hanging open.

"What?" I asked.

"No offense," said Robbyn, "but you don't seem like the type."

"What type is that?"

"The type to put up with a dominant male. You're too independent."

"We do have some issues."

"Like what?" Brooke asked, with genuine interest.

"Well, he doesn't like it when I take risks."

"That sounds caring," said Brooke.

"And sometimes I bend the law a little. That really pisses him off."

"It's all about control," said Robbyn. "Cops need to be in control. That's why they're cops."

"Not all of them," I said defensively. "Bill's usually pretty mellow, and he became a cop because he wanted to make a difference."

Robbyn still looked skeptical, so I told

them the story about Bill's rock band that had gone on tour when he was a teenager, the bunko artist who had tried to bilk them out of their meager savings, the cop who had worked the case, and Bill's subsequent decision to become a police cadet. They both listened with rapt attention. These two loved a good story.

When I'd finished my tale, I said, "Anyway, my point is that if you find Faulkner attractive you shouldn't let the fact that he's a cop get in the way."

Brooke blushed again and looked down into her coffee cup. "You know my history with men," she said.

Robbyn nodded, but said, "There's no point in dwelling on the past, sugar. Everyone makes mistakes. Hell, I wish I had a nickel for every man I shouldn't have slept with. But Nikki's right. You should take a shot at Faulkner. If you don't, I will."

Brooke looked at her cousin. "You're leaving on Sunday."

"Yeah, but we could have one hell of a weekend. Besides, I don't really *have* to be home until September. I was thinking I might stay a few more weeks."

"That would be wonderful," said Brooke.

"I have an idea," I interrupted. "Why

don't we take Faulkner out to dinner tonight after the meeting? Then you can both flirt with him and see who he responds to."

"Sounds like fun," said Robbyn.

"Okay," Brooke said. "But he'll pick Robbyn. Men love Robbyn."

"Don't sell yourself short, honey," said Robbyn. "You're not exactly chopped liver."

We spent the whole day at the apartment, and at 7:00 both women changed into what they thought were appropriate outfits for an orchid club meeting. Robbyn put on her new outfit from Neiman's, and Brooke wore a pair of rose-colored slacks with a cream silk tank top. I was in Eddie Bauer cargo shorts, a red short sleeved cotton blouse, and running shoes.

Chapter 27

We rolled into the San Mateo Garden Center lot at 7:45, and found Faulkner waiting for us. He was leaning casually against his beat-up Chevy and puffing on a cigar.

"*Stud-muffin alert,*" murmured Robbyn under her breath.

Brooke punched her in the arm and whispered, "Hush!"

I scanned the parking lot for a VW van, but didn't see one.

"Good evening, Detective," I said, as I locked Buddy in the car.

"Ms. Hunter." He nodded at Brooke and Robbyn. "Ladies."

I wondered if greeting me separately was intended to imply that I was *not* a lady, but dismissed the thought as irrelevant.

"You ever get that safe open?" I asked.

"As a matter of fact we did."

"And?"

"And we'll be bringing Archer back in for additional questioning."

"Excellent. Did you listen to the tape?"

"Yes. Even though we can't use it, it's good background information."

"You're welcome," I said.

Faulkner smirked and put out his cigar in a tall standing ashtray.

"Have you had dinner?" I asked, as we stepped inside.

"Not really. I grabbed a vending machine sandwich around two. Why do you ask?"

"I was thinking, since you've been so nice about sharing information, that maybe we could take you out for a bite after the meeting."

Faulkner smiled. "You buying?"

"I am," I said, thinking he might be reluctant to accept if he knew I'd be adding the dinner tab to my expense sheet.

The meeting room was filled with an interesting assortment of people. Some looked like professional gardeners, some like housewives. There were a few older men, and a couple of women who looked like they belonged on the society page. In the back of the room was a long table with a coffee urn and a basket labeled N*on-Member Contributions*. I took out my wallet and dropped a twenty into the basket.

Brooke, Robbyn, and Faulkner took chairs in the back row while I strolled forward looking for someone in charge. Seated in the front of the room were two men and two women whom I guessed were the panel of experts invited to speak tonight. A tall distinguished looking man stood near a podium to the right of the panel. I approached and introduced myself. His name was Randolph Curtis. I asked if I could make a brief announcement during tonight's meeting. I told him about Stanley's death and his stolen hybrid, then took out the journal and the identikit picture.

"I was sorry to hear about Mr. Godard's passing," he said. "He was a brilliant horticulturist."

"Do you recognize this man?" I asked, handing him a copy of the identikit sketch.

He furrowed his brow. "He looks familiar, but I couldn't tell you his name."

My pulse quickened. "Did Stanley discuss his new hybrid at the meetings?"

"Not openly, but he did mention it to me. He was quite excited."

"Could someone have overheard your conversation?"

"I imagine so."

"Did you discuss it with anyone else?"

"Certainly not," he huffed.

"Sorry. I didn't mean to offend you, but the hybrid was stolen the same day Stanley was killed, so there may be a connection."

"That's a tragedy," said Curtis, a little abruptly. "I need to call the meeting to order. You may make your announcement after the panel discussion."

"Thank you," I said, and handed him one of my business cards in case he forgot my name.

I scanned faces as I walked toward the back of the room. I didn't see anyone with long hair and a beard, but that didn't mean he wasn't here. It's easy to change your appearance. My gaze settled on a man standing near the door, wearing sunglasses. His hair was brown, short, and wiry, and he was clean-shaven; wearing Bermuda shorts, a Hawaiian shirt, and sneakers. The sunglasses, and the fact that he'd positioned himself near the exit, got my attention.

I slid past Faulkner into the back row and plunked myself down next to Robbyn, who had, I assumed, made certain that Brooke was seated next to "the hottie."

Curtis called the meeting to order and everyone took seats, except the guy in the back, who hovered near the coffee urn. Having him behind me made the skin on the back of my neck crawl. Not a good sign. I was tempted to sneak outside and search the lot for the VW van, but I knew Jim would be arriving at 9:00. If the van was there, he'd find it.

The panel was introduced and the guy in sunglasses took his coffee and perched on a vacant chair at the end of our row. I scribbled a note to Faulkner, telling him where the man was sitting and asking him to keep an eye on him when I went up to make my announcement.

Each person on the panel gave a brief lecture followed by a question and answer period.

By nine o'clock I found myself struggling to stay alert and was considering getting a cup of coffee from the urn when I heard my name. I looked up at Curtis, who motioned me forward. Embarrassed by my inability to remain focused, I skirted past Robbyn, Brooke, and Faulkner, glanced casually at the sunglasses guy, and strode to the front of the room.

"Thank you," I said to Curtis, as I moved behind the lectern.

"My name is Nicoli Hunter," I began. "I'm a private investigator and I'm here because I need your help."

I told them about Stanley's murder, and heard a few muted gasps. Then I informed them about the stolen hybrid, which elicited several startled exclamations. Apparently this crowd was more moved by the loss of an orchid than the death of one of their members.

"Although the hybrid was stolen," I continued. "Stanley's notes on the process were left behind." I took the journal out of my purse and showed it to the group, glancing at the man in the back as I did so. He was on his feet now, his sunglasses pointed in my direction. I replaced the book in my bag and held up the identikit sketch. "We think this man may be involved." I handed a stack of identikit copies to a man in the front row. "Could you pass these out please?"

I gave Faulkner a look and he got up and moved toward the door.

I returned to the podium. "I'm hoping

one of you will be able to identify this man," I said. "He drives an old orange VW van and he may recently have changed his appearance."

I watched the members' faces as the pictures were passed around. One woman looked sharply at me after glancing at the sketch. She nodded slightly, then turned to look around the room, stopping when she saw the man in the Hawaiian shirt. She turned back to me and nodded again.

Faulkner was blocking the exit and the sunglasses guy looked nervous. His attention was divided between me and Faulkner, his head rotating back and forth between us. Then he approached the coffee urn and refilled his cup. I realized what he was planning and hoped Faulkner had seen it too.

"I'll be in back after the meeting," I said, "if anyone wants to talk to me."

The man in the back was moving toward the door as I rushed down the aisle. I was halfway there when he threw the scalding hot coffee into Faulkner's face, shoved him aside, and bolted out the door. Faulkner covered his seared face with his hands and bent at the waist.

I tossed my purse to Brooke as I ran

toward the door. "Stay here," I shouted over my shoulder.

I hit the parking lot at a jog, unzipping my fanny pack holster as I ran. I drew the Ruger and paused, listening for the sound of feet pounding the pavement or an engine starting. Instead all I heard was barking. Buddy was sounding the alarm. He'd remembered the guy's scent from Stanley's greenhouse and the Whole Foods garage. I took out my cell and speed dialed Jim.

"Sutherland."

"Are you here?"

"Yeah. What's up?"

"A guy just ran out of the building. Short brown hair, clean-shaven, wearing shorts and a Hawaiian shirt. Where are you?"

"I'm on the street, and your man just passed me."

"On foot?"

"Yes."

"Follow him, but be careful. He's probably armed."

"Gotcha."

I heard Jim's engine catch through the cell and started running toward the street. When I reached the sidewalk I turned both ways, but there was no sign of the man or of Jim's Honda. I headed south and heard two gunshots in stereo through the cell and maybe a block away to the west.

"Jim!"

"I'm okay. Son of a bitch shot out my tire. I'm pursuing on foot."

I ran toward the sound of the shots. "Keep your distance," I shouted into the phone, "but try to get his plate number."

"He's in the van," said Jim, breathing hard now. "There's mud on the rear plate."

I rounded a corner and saw Jim positioned behind a Sycamore, his Tokarev automatic in his hand. The VW van was ten yards away moving toward the intersection. I kept running, grateful for all the hours I'd spent on the treadmill. The van was sputtering and coughing but still pulling away from me. I raised the Ruger, took aim, and fired at one of the rear tires. I hit the bumper. Maybe I should spend more time at the firing range and less at the gym.

The van's windows were down and as it made a right hand turn I saw the muzzle flash and ducked just as a bullet zinged over my head. I hit the ground and the van disappeared around the corner. I couldn't believe he'd gotten away from me, again.

Jim and I left his wounded Honda parked on the street and walked back to the garden center. We went inside and found Brooke applying a cold compress to Faulkner's face. The room was in an uproar.

The woman who had nodded at me during the meeting approached. "Did you catch him?" she asked.

"No. He got away."

"I always knew there was something wrong with that man."

"I don't suppose you know his name."

"I don't remember his first name, but his last name is Cross. I remember it because he always seems angry. I thought the name was appropriate."

"Bernard Cross?"

"Yes, that's it!"

I turned to Faulkner. "How are you doing?"

"He needs to go to the hospital," said Brooke.

"I'm okay," said Faulkner. "I closed my eyes just in time."

He pulled the wet towel away from his face, which was swollen, red, and blotchy.

"You look like hell," I said. "I think Brooke is right. You need to see a doctor."

"Later," said Faulkner.

"The guy got away after shooting out Jim's

tire. He also took a shot at me and missed. We have a name though. Bernard Cross."

Faulkner took out his cell. "I need to call this in."

CHAPTER 28

THE SAN MATEO PD ARRIVED and took statements from everyone, then examined Jim's car. They agreed to allow Faulkner to impound the car, even though it wasn't his jurisdiction, so the bullet in the tire could be compared to the one that had killed Stanley Godard. I was sure the ballistics would match.

Brooke and I finally convinced Faulkner that he needed medical attention. We eased him into the passenger seat of his Chevy and Brooke drove him to the San Mateo Medical Center on 39th Avenue. Robbyn, Buddy, and I followed in my car.

While Faulkner was in with the doctor, Buddy and I waited outside the emergency room entrance. I lit a cigarette and called Bill to tell him what was happening. He sounded distracted and I knew without asking that he was involved up to his eyeballs in the search for Nina Jezek.

By the time Faulkner had been treated and his face and neck coated with goo, it was almost 11:00.

"You must be starving," I said, as we all stepped outside.

"I am, but I need to run Cross for priors and see if I can get an address."

"Can't that wait an hour?" Brooke asked. "You need to eat."

He looked at her through his swollen eyelids and I caught the spark of interest. "Maybe I have time for a burger," he said.

Brooke insisted on driving Faulkner, so Robbyn and I took my car to the nearest fast food joint. We went inside and placed our orders. Faulkner was on the phone the whole time, so Brooke took the liberty of ordering him a chef salad instead of a burger. I ordered two cheeseburgers; one for me and one for Buddy. We collected our food and sat down at a table near the window so I could keep an eye on the parking lot, my dog, and my BMW.

Faulkner looked disconsolately at his salad and said, "Cross has two priors for aggravated assault and a sealed juvenile record. According to the DVM, he lives at 4333 Olympic Avenue." His eyes locked onto the burger I was eating, then moved hungrily to Buddy's still wrapped burger.

"Wait a minute," I said. "I know that address. That's the San Mateo Bowling Center. They're one of my clients." I remembered my theory that Cross lived in his van. Maybe he parked in the Bowling Center lot at night. Or maybe he worked there. I knew they were open until 1:00 a.m. on Fridays. I checked my watch. It was 11:20.

I shared my thoughts with Faulkner as he picked at his salad. He was still eyeing Buddy's burger so I went and got a plastic knife from the utensil bin, cut mine in half, and handed over the untouched portion.

He said, "Thanks," took a huge bite and mumbled, "Maybe we should stop by the bowling alley and take a look around. See if anyone recognizes the picture."

"Good idea," I said.

"Eat your salad," said Brooke.

Faulkner finished the last bite of burger and forked up some lettuce and ham. Robbyn winked at me.

Before we left the restaurant I tossed the bun, tomato, and pickles from Buddy's burger into the trash. Wheat gives him a rash, tomatoes are bad for dogs, and he doesn't like pickles. I quickly fed him, gave him half a bottle of water, and then used the rest of the water to rinse my hands.

By the time we pulled into the Bowling Center lot it was close to midnight. There were several cars in the lot, but the van wasn't among them.

I called Faulkner on my cell. "I'm going to drive around the block and check the side streets. Don't go inside until I get back. I have a stack of those identikit pictures in my bag."

He saluted me through the car window and closed his phone, turning to face Brooke.

I pulled back onto the street and Robbyn said, "I told you so."

"What?"

"She really likes him, and now that he's injured, her maternal instincts have kicked in. That man doesn't stand a chance."

"You're right," I said. I was thinking that they could both do a lot worse.

I circled the block searching for the VW van, drove up and down a couple of alleys, and eventually gave up and returned to the lot in front of the bowling alley, where Brooke and Faulkner were waiting for us.

As Faulkner stepped out of the Chevy I saw that he was on his cell again. He turned to me as he ended the call.

"We got ballistics back on the round that hit your friend's tire." He lowered his voice as he continued. "It doesn't match the slug that killed Godard. Doesn't mean Cross isn't our killer. He might have more than one gun."

"Huh," I said. I know, eloquent.

We entered the Bowling Center and split up, showing the identikit drawing to all the employees in the bar, the restaurant, and the bowling alley. I waited in line behind a couple of bowlers who were paying for games and shoes, then approached the middle-aged woman who manned the counter. Her name tag read Deanna.

I presented the drawing, took out my PI license, and asked, "Do you recognize this man?"

Deanna's eyebrows rose as she gazed at the picture, then her wide eyes met mine. "He's the night janitor, Bernie Cross. Why, has he done something wrong?"

"We just need to speak with him. What hours does he work?"

"I'm not sure when he leaves, but he

comes in a little before one a.m., when we close."

"Does Bernie drive a VW van?"

"Why yes. How did you know that?"

"He was seen in the area of an explosion last Saturday. We just need to ask him if he saw anything. Please don't tell him I was looking for him. I don't want to scare him off."

Deanna nodded mutely, then turned to a team of bowlers who were waiting impatiently behind me.

I found Faulkner in the bar holding a glass of ice water against his face and wincing. Brooke and Robbyn were sitting at the table with him and they all had frustrated looks on their faces.

"What's wrong?" I asked.

"Nobody we talked to admits to knowing Cross," Faulkner said.

"Well, the woman at the rental counter knows him. Bernard Cross is the night janitor here. Did I tell you he's registered to exhibit a new breed of orchid at the Santa Barbara show this weekend?"

Faulkner shook his head and grimaced.

"Deanna said he comes in a little before one." I checked my watch. "We have forty-five minutes to kill. Does anybody want to bowl?"

Robbyn and Brooke both raised their hands and bounced in their seats like a couple of school kids, chanting, "I do, I do!"

Faulkner laughed, then winced again.

"Did the ER doctor give you anything for the pain?" I asked.

"Yeah, but I need to stay sharp."

"Well, since you're in too much pain to roll a ball, how about you keep score for us?"

"I can do that." He smiled at Brooke. She blushed and quickly looked away.

"Right," I said. "Let's go rent some ugly shoes."

The cousins and I had a wonderful time bowling, although none of us were any good. There were a lot of gutter balls, and a lot of laughter. Faulkner kept track of our scores, and kept looking at his watch. At 12:45 I approached Deanna, who was still working the counter.

"What entrance does Bernie use," I asked her, as I returned my rented shoes.

"Back door," she pointed toward the far right hand lanes. "There's a store room back there, and a locked door to the parking lot."

"Thank you, Deanna."

I returned to Faulkner and the girls, and pointed out the door to the storage room.

"We should probably try to catch him outside if we can," Faulkner said.

The establishment was emptying of patrons, except for the bar where a few teams were still hoisting beers. Brooke and Robbyn quickly returned their bowling shoes to Deanna. As we exited through the front I asked them to wait in my car with Buddy. After Faulkner squelched their objections they did as I asked, and he and I rounded the building, looking for an appropriate hiding place near the back door. Luckily, there was a dumpster to the right of the rear entrance. We'd just stepped behind the stinky container when I heard the rattle trap VW enter the lot.

I put a hand on Faulkner's arm and nodded, letting him know what that sound was. He pulled his Glock out of its holster and whispered, "Stay here."

I nodded and covertly slipped my hand into my fanny pack, releasing the snap on the internal holster. We heard the van engine rattle to a stop, and the slam of a car door. Faulkner inched his way closer to the back door of the bowling alley, his muscles tensed, the Glock at his side pointing toward the ground. I stayed behind, my Ruger at the ready in case he needed back-up.

We listened to shuffling steps approaching our hiding place, and then Faulkner stepped out into the open, raising his weapon.

"Bernard Cross," he shouted. "Stop where you are. Hands on your head."

I had a feeling Cross would be uncooperative, so I moved swiftly around the other side of the dumpster and stepped up behind him. When he turned away from Faulkner to make a run for his van, I executed a roundhouse kick, knocking him on his ass. Faulkner cuffed his hands behind his back while muttering under his breath that he'd told me to stay put.

"Yeah, I heard you," I said. "And you're welcome, again."

Once Faulkner had handcuffed Cross, I reached into his jacket pocket and snatched the keys to his van. Before Faulkner could stop me, I'd unlocked the side door of the van and leaned inside. Stanley's prized orchid hybrid was nestled between two small pillows in a sturdy wooden box. I leaned in and carefully lifted the box out.

Faulkner stood next to me, and I said, "I'd like to show this to Brooke, if you don't mind." He did mind, but I went ahead anyway, and Brooke was able to identify the stolen orchid.

I asked Robbyn to give Buddy a quick walk when they got back to Brooke's condo, and Faulkner and I escorted Cross, and the orchid, to the San Carlos Police station in the Chevy.

Chapter 29

Nina spent Wednesday and Thursday studying her next target. This one would be more difficult. He appeared nervous, always looking over his shoulder or checking the rear view mirrors of the luxury car he drove. Nina decided to rent a second car and wear a wig when she followed him on Friday.

He worked at a firm in San Carlos that was inaccessible, his house in the Belmont Hills was gated, and he didn't use a cleaning service. This was a very private man. His background showed that he'd never been married or even engaged, which was not surprising, but many wealthy and active pedophiles dated at least occasionally, in order to appear normal.

Early Friday morning Nina donned a red pixie cut wig and drove her new rental car to San Carlos. She hoped that her prey would arrive before the other employees, but even if there were a few around, they'd be unable to identify her later. By 10:00 a.m. he still hadn't entered the lot. She considered going to his house and attempting to gain entry, even though it was likely to be equipped with an alarm system.

By noon her frustration level compelled her to move forward. She drove to the Belmont Hills address and parked her rental car on the street above his house. She looked through her binoculars, scanning the grounds for any weakness, but the fence appeared to be continuous. There was only one possibility. An old oak tree stood close enough to the fence to be used as a jumping off point. Nina climbed out of the rental car and took a walk.

Picking her way carefully down the hill through the rich vegetation, Nina made her way to the oak. It was just close enough to the fence, and some of the branches were low. She tossed a twig at the fence, tensing instinctively at the spark of electricity the contact caused. Interesting. The grounds were surrounded with an electrified fence. Nina wondered if the extreme security measures were intended to keep prowlers out, or to keep victims from escaping.

This man's most recent purchase from Fredo Giordano had been only four months ago. There was a possibility the little girl was still alive, and somewhere inside the house. That would complicate things, since Nina planned to kill the man. No one would be able to get onto the property if they were looking for him so, if the child was trapped inside, no one would find her.

Nina climbed back up the hill to the rental car, and waited.

As the sun began to set she once again trained her binoculars on the house, and sure enough, lights began to come on. First in what appeared to be an office, then in the kitchen windows.

Nina drove to a restaurant in downtown Belmont, ordered a crab salad, and used the facilities. She ate some of the salad, drank a glass of water, and paid her tab.

Returning to the hillside above the house she continued watching until only one light remained on. A second floor room she assumed was a bedroom. When that light finally went out, she slipped on her gloves, checked her pockets, making sure the taser and switchblade were with her, and climbed down the hill again. It was 2:00 a.m., and the neighborhood was silent.

Nina had no difficulty climbing the oak tree and dropped to the ground inside the fenced yard with ease. She'd always been athletic. She moved around the periphery of the yard, staying in the shadows near the fence until she was close to a pair of French doors. No motion-activated flood lights came on. Nina used a mini flashlight to check the door frames, looking for wires and cameras, but there didn't appear to be any alarm or surveillance systems in place. Maybe the owner considered the electrified fence and locked gate security enough.

She withdrew a small set of lock picks from her back pocket and went to work. Three minutes later she was inside. Using the flashlight she found her way to the stairs. She climbed them slowly, staying close to the wall to avoid treading on any squeaky steps. When she'd reached the landing she used her light briefly to locate the room she assumed was the predator's bedroom. Her blood began to thrum as she approached his lair. Moving swiftly now, in case she'd triggered a silent alarm, Nina pulled the taser out of her jacket pocket and held it ready.

The bedroom door was unlocked. She eased it open and moved into the room, leaving the door open behind her. A bedside lamp illuminated the sleeping man. Nina was at his side in a flash and pressed the taser to his exposed chest. The man jerked awake, breaking the connection, and lunged under his pillow retrieving a Sig Sauer P220. Nina pushed his gun hand aside and leaned back in with the taser, but the first jolt had only made the big man twitchy. He quickly raised the gun and fired before she could move out of the way. Luckily his aim was off, and he only nicked her left shoulder. Nina snatched the gun out of his hand and shot Geoffrey Archer pointblank in the forehead. Blood and brain matter drenched the pillows behind him.

Nina tossed the gun on the floor and was about to make her escape when she heard a child crying softly somewhere nearby. She turned in a slow circle trying to identify where the sound was coming from. There were two closed doors in the bedroom. Nina opened the first to find a huge walk-in closet, complete with a mirrored dressing area. The second door revealed the master bathroom. The sound of crying grew faint as she entered the lavish bathroom, so she went back into the closet. Moving beyond the dressing area she found another door, this one locked. She rattled the doorknob and the crying abruptly stopped.

Nina went back into Archer's bedroom and searched the pockets of the pants he'd draped over a chair. She located his keys and returned to the closet. She tried each key until she found the one that fit the lock, and eased open the door.

What she saw made her blood run cold, and she wished Archer was still alive so she could kill him again. A small Asian girl was curled in a tight ball of fear in the corner of the room. She appeared to be around eight years old. The room also contained a princess-style child's bed, complete with a gauzy pink canopy. Several stuffed animals lay atop the bed, but the terrified child held no toy to comfort herself. She stared at Nina, a look of disbelief on her tearstained face.

"Do you speak English?" Nina asked.

"Yes. I learn English in orphanage," the child replied, her voice trembling.

"Good. The man who hurt you is dead. I'm going to get you out of here, but I need a minute to cover my shoulder first. Do you understand?" Nina knew her HIV positive blood was a danger to anyone who came in contact with it, and the last thing she wanted to do was cause additional harm to this helpless child.

"I understand," came the soft reply.

Nina found a heavy Gortex jacket and pulled it on over her wounded shoulder. The waterproof fabric would keep the blood inside the jacket. She zipped it up to her neck, cinched it with a drawstring at the hips, and tightened the Velcro cuff straps around her wrists.

Nina returned to the child, who wore a pink, baby-doll nightgown. "Do you have any other clothes?" she asked.

Chapter 30

This time Faulkner allowed me to be in the interview room with him; probably because it was the middle of the night and no one else would know. Cross was cuffed to a bracket set into the steel table. As his venomous glare settled on me I realized that he had a wandering eye. That explained the description we'd gotten from Kopelin. Cross's eyes appeared to be looking in different directions. That wasn't creepy at all.

Faulkner began the questions by asking about the day of Stanley's death. He asked Cross why he'd been at Stanley's office. Cross turned his angry gaze on Faulkner, but said nothing.

"You might as well confess," Faulkner said. "We know you broke into Godard's greenhouse and swiped his hybrid orchid, and we know you were at his office when he was shot and killed. The DA will go easier on you if you cooperate."

Cross finally spoke. His voice was an incongruous soft, velvety baritone. "I didn't kill him," he said, his eyes filled with malice. "I just wanted to make sure he was in his office before I went to his house. All I wanted was the damn plant."

Elizabeth had been right!

"Okay," Faulkner said. "Tell me what happened."

"I knocked on the back door of his office. I was gonna hide behind a bush and wait to see if he answered his door, but then I heard the gunshot and I got the hell out of there."

"Wait," I said. "You knocked on the door and then you heard a gunshot?"

"Isn't that what I just said?"

I turned to Faulkner. "Where have I heard this before?" It was Archer's story all over again, but from a different angle.

"Anyway," Cross continued, "I ran back to my van and took off. This asshole in a Mercedes almost broadsided me coming out of Godard's lot. If he was in that office with Godard, *he's* who you should be looking at."

"Fine," said Faulkner. "Then what did you do?"

"I went to Godard's place and broke into the greenhouse. I searched both the greenhouse and the house, but I couldn't find his journal. I knew he kept one, because he used to bring it to meetings with him, but I couldn't find the damn thing, so I just took the orchid and left. Then *you*," he said, turning back to me, "showed up with his journal. Where the hell did *you* get it?" He spit out the words with obvious rage.

I said nothing.

"Why did you shoot at the man who followed you from the Garden Center?" Faulkner asked.

Cross thought about that for a minute before he said, "I was afraid he was trying to steal the orchid from me."

"Seriously?" I asked. "Is that also why you took a shot at me?"

"I want a lawyer," Cross said, and that was the end of the interrogation.

We left Cross alone in the interview room, and Faulkner led me to a break room where he made a fresh pot of coffee.

"You want a cup?"

"Oh *God*, yes," I said. "We need to take another run at Archer."

"What do you mean *we*?"

"Hey, you wouldn't even have known about Archer and Cross if it wasn't for me."

"What's your point?"

"You owe me, Faulkner. I promised Brooke I'd try to find out who killed Stanley. If Cross is telling the truth, then it was Archer who shot Stanley in the head and blew up his office. There were probably just a few bills in that suitcase along with the bomb, and when Cross knocked on the back door, Archer panicked, shot Stanley, and ran. The bomb might have been on a timer, or he might have used a remote detonator, but he's the guy. Do you have a home address for him?"

"I do, but I'm not going to give it to you."

Feeling enormously frustrated, I allowed Faulkner to send me home in a squad car. At least the uniform assigned to drive me allowed me to sit in the front seat. As we pulled out of the SCPD garage I remembered Brooke and Robbyn had my car and my dog, so I asked the uniform if he'd take me to Redwood Shores. He didn't have a problem with that, since it was closer than the marina anyway.

Once we were on the road I pulled out

my cell and called Brooke. A quick glance at my watch told me it was 2:30 in the morning.

Brooke picked up on the fourth ring, sounding sleepy.

"Nikki? What's going on?"

"Sorry to wake you, Brooke. I need to get Buddy and my car back. I hope you don't mind if I drop by long enough to pick them up."

"Of course not. Should I make coffee?"

"No, don't bother. I'll fill you and Robbyn in on everything in the morning."

"Okay. When will you be here?"

We'd just exited the freeway.

"Maybe three minutes?"

"Okay," she said, and disconnected.

Poor baby, with all that had been happening she must be exhausted.

The uniform dropped me in the lot of Brooke's complex. I thanked him politely for the ride, and entered Brooke's building. I still had an adrenaline rush going from the take-down at the bowling alley, and jogged up to the second floor landing. Brooke opened the door before I could knock.

She had my keys in her hand. Buddy nudged her aside so he could get to me, and stood up on his hind legs, putting his forepaws on my shoulders, the better to wash my face. Being a gracious Southern belle, Brooke asked if I'd like to come in.

"No thanks," I said, accepting my key ring. "I'm sure Jim is somewhere in your lot, in a new nondescript car, keeping an eye on you. I'll see you in the morning."

My cell rang before I made it down the steps.

"Who's your new chauffer?" Jim asked, a smile in his voice.

"I didn't get his name or his badge number. I had to lend Brooke my car after we caught Cross, so I could sit in on the interview with Faulkner. Bullet wasn't a match, by the way."

"Wait, you caught the guy? Where?"

"San Mateo Bowling Center. He's the night janitor."

"Good job. I assume he's being held for shooting out my tire."

"And for stealing Stanley's orchid. He's in lock-up at the SCPD at the moment. He insists he didn't kill Stanley, but just knocked on his back door to make sure he was there. Says he heard a gunshot immediately after knocking, so he took off."

"You believe him?"

"It doesn't matter what I believe. We need to take another look at Archer, and

Faulkner won't give me his home address. When I get back to the office I'll wake my friend Michael up and see if he can get it for me."

"You're not planning on confronting Archer alone are you?"

"Um, no, probably not."

"Be careful, Nikki."

"You betcha. See you in the morning."

Chapter 31

I drove to the marina and, after a quick walk, Buddy and I unlocked the office. Buddy drank some water from his bowl and sank to the ground, instantly asleep. I wish I had that ability.

I tossed my fanny pack onto one of the visitor's chairs and speed dialed my friend Michael, white hat hacker extraordinaire, and listened as his phone rang once then was picked up by voicemail. *Damn!*

"Hey, Michael, it's Nikki. I need a home address on Geoffrey Archer. I don't have a social, but he's a CFO at a pharmaceutical research company on Old County Road in San Carlos." I left a brief description of Archer, then replaced the phone in the cradle.

As I turned toward the windows I caught

movement out of the corner of my eye and realized I hadn't locked the office door behind me. A woman stood just inside the doorway. Five-foot-nine, maybe a hundred and thirty pounds. It was hard to tell because she was wearing a heavy jacket that was too big on her. She had short red hair and brown eyes, and she was standing next to a little Asian girl who was dressed only in an oversized cable knit sweater, the sleeves rolled up to accommodate her diminutive stature. The red-haired woman was holding the little girl's hand, and they were both staring intently at me.

What the fuck?

"Can I help you?" I asked, not knowing what else to say. For Christ's sake, it was three in the *morning*!

"We need your help," the woman said.

I heard Buddy growl low in his throat, and turned in his direction. "Buddy, stay," I said, hoping that for once he would obey. Something about the woman's voice was familiar to me, and I felt a rush of adrenaline as I began to put the pieces together. Nina was back in town and had begun killing again. She would have changed her appearance. The woman in front of me had a child with her who was clearly not her daughter.

"Oh my God. *Nina?*"

I stood up, moving toward my fanny pack and the Ruger, but it was on the other side of the desk. Nina dropped the child's hand and quickly moved to intercept me. She had her stun gun out before I took two steps.

"Please don't make me taser you again," she said. "I'm not here to hurt you."

The Ruger was in my fanny pack, but I remembered I'd stowed the Glock in the holster under my lap drawer. I could have it out in a nanosecond if need be. I sat back down in my desk chair, taking in the situation. Buddy came over and stood next to me, looking curiously at our two visitors. I grabbed onto his collar to keep him away from Nina and her taser.

"Where did you find her?" I asked, nodding at the child who was, once again, clinging to her hand.

"That's not important. Her name is Caifen. She's an eight-year-old who was kidnapped, or maybe purchased, from an orphanage in Guizhou. I need you to contact child protective services and make sure she's taken care of. Tell them to send a woman to pick her up. She's been through a lot. She'll need counseling, by a *female* therapist. Think you can handle all of that?"

I almost laughed at Nina's sarcastic sense of humor. If I was being honest with myself, I admired this woman for her mission, if not for her methods.

"Probably," I said. "Why did you bring Caifen to me?"

"I couldn't very well take her to the police, now could I? I respect Bill Anderson. If he's in a relationship with you it's a safe bet you're not a complete idiot."

"Do you have Giordano's client list?" I asked.

"How do you know about that?"

"FBI."

She nodded. "Look, I'm not here to answer your questions or to bond with you. I have to go now. Please don't try to stop me."

I had the Glock in my hand and pointed at Nina in a heartbeat. She stepped away from the child and held her hands out in front of her. "You don't want to do that. I'm HIV positive. If you shoot me, the blood spatter will hit Caifen. It might even hit you at this range."

The little girl looked up at Nina, then looked at me holding a gun on her hero, and began to cry. She dropped to the floor and curled into a tight ball, sobbing inconsolably. The sound almost broke my heart. Based on Nina's history of targeting pedophiles, I had a pretty good idea what this unfortunate child had endured. I really didn't want to make it worse. While all of these thoughts were running through my mind, my eyes trained on Caifen, Nina had slipped out the door and vanished. I hate when that happens.

I released Buddy's collar, walked to the open door and looked out at the marina grounds, then closed and locked the door and turned back to Caifen. Buddy stayed by my side for the moment, but looked inquisitively at the child.

"This is my dog, Buddy," I said. "He's a very good dog. You aren't afraid of dogs are you?"

Caifen shook her head, now watching Buddy, who was wagging his tail and sniffing the air around her. I sat down on the floor next to her and said, "Buddy come." It was the one command he regularly obeyed.

My pup stepped forward and nuzzled the little girl's ear, then gave her face a single lick. She wrapped her arms around his neck and began to sob again. Buddy allowed himself to be hugged, occasionally licking the tears from her cheeks as she continued to cry. I grabbed the Kleenex box off my desk and set it on the floor beside her.

"Are you hungry?" I asked.

She turned her red-rimmed eyes in my direction and nodded.

I checked the mini-fridge in my kitchenette and came back with a boysenberry yogurt, a spoon, and a bottle of spring water. While Caifen was eating I called Bill's cell and woke him up.

"Hey, babe. Where are you?"

"I'm in the office. Are you at home or on the boat?"

"I'm on the boat. I was hoping we'd get a chance to see each other tonight. What the hell time is it anyway?"

"It's after three. Can you come up to the office, please?"

"What's wrong? Are you okay?"

"I'm fine, but I just had a close encounter of the Nina variety, and she left me something to remember her by."

"Holy shit! Do you need me to call dispatch?"

"Nope. Just come to the office, please."

"On my way."

I turned back to Caifen and saw that she was holding the yogurt container in both hands as Buddy licked it clean.

Two minutes later Bill approached my locked office doors. I opened them and ushered the man in my life inside, wrapping my arms around him for a brief moment before locking the doors again.

Bill was staring at the child huddled on my floor next to Buddy, and she was staring back at him, her eyes wide with fear.

"Caifen, this is my friend Bill. He's a police officer, and he won't hurt you. Okay?"

The tiny waif nodded once, then turned her attention back to Buddy.

Bill and I stepped into the kitchenette and I explained what had happened.

When I'd finished he said, "So she's a brown-eyed redhead now?"

"I think she was wearing a wig. Her face looks totally different, though. Unrecognizable, really."

"Well shit. I guess we'd better call child protective services and get someone over here to take care of Caifen."

"Ask for a woman, please." I nodded toward the child on the floor still hanging onto my dog. "She's going to be afraid of men for a long time."

Bill nodded and pulled his cell from his pants pocket. While he made the call I sat back down on the floor and gently rubbed

Caifen's back. She sniffled softly and turned to face me. I handed her a tissue and she quietly blew her nose.

"Thank you," she whispered, holding the tissue in one tiny fist, and gripping Buddy's collar with the other, afraid if she let go he might slip away. Buddy eased his ninety-five pound frame down onto the floor and placed his head in her lap. Canine therapy.

Bill finished his call and said he was going outside to meet the woman from child protective services in the parking lot. I locked eyes with him, wondering if there was any possibility Nina was still nearby.

"Be careful," I said.

He nodded as he went out the door. "Lock this behind me."

So he'd had the same thought. I got up and locked the office doors, then returned to my kitchenette and made a pot of coffee. I had to be back at Brooke's condo in about four hours. It looked like I wouldn't be getting any sleep tonight.

Bill was back ten minutes later with the matronly CPS woman in tow. I unlocked the doors yet again, ushered then inside, and offered coffee.

"Coffee sounds wonderful. I'm Melinda

Tentrees," she said, extending her hand. "And you're Nikki Hunter, correct?"

I shook her hand, which was soft, warm, and surprisingly strong. "I am," I said. "How do you take your coffee?"

"Black is fine, thanks."

Before returning to the coffee maker I stooped down next to Caifen and said, "Caifen, this is Melinda. She's here to help you, okay?"

Caifen was still seated on the floor with Buddy. She glanced up at Melinda for a moment, then turned her tear-stained face toward me. "May I have another yogurt, please? Buddy ate mine."

I laughed and went to retrieve the last yogurt from my fridge before pouring three cups of coffee. Bill seated himself at my desk and watched as Melinda moved to sit on the floor a few yards away from Buddy and Caifen. She was being sensitive to the little girl's fear. Giving her space. *Excellent.*

An hour later our coffee cups were empty, Caifen had finished her yogurt, and had shared her bottle of water with Buddy. There was a puddle of water on the carpet, but it was a small price to pay. Melinda had slowly moved closer to the child, and eventually reached out to touch her hand.

Caifen had stiffened momentarily, until Buddy gave Melinda's hand a lick, and then the little girl had relaxed.

They were getting ready to leave when Caifen asked if she could use the bathroom. I looked at Melinda who nodded. I escorted the waif to my office restroom, and Buddy insisted on going inside with her. Fine with me, and it seemed to make her feel safe as long as he was nearby.

"That dog of yours could do some real good at the local children's hospital," Melinda said when I came out of the hallway.

"I'd never thought about that, but I suppose you're right. He's great with kids."

We heard the flush, and then water running. I wondered how long it had been since the little girl had been allowed to bathe. How long since she'd been cared for. Not only had she lost her parents, she'd been abducted by monsters who had taken her to a foreign country and sold her to a child molester. Not for the first time I wondered if Nina had the right idea.

Caifen and Buddy came out of the bathroom, and Melinda held out her hand, waiting patiently for Caifen to respond. Finally the child gave Buddy one last, lingering hug, kissed him on the nose, and put her tiny hand in Melinda's. Before they could get out the door I handed Melinda one of my business cards and asked that she keep me posted on what was happening with Caifen.

"Maybe she and Buddy can have a play date sometime soon," I added.

Melinda smiled, looked down at the little girl who was now in her charge, and said, "I think that could be arranged. Thank you, Nikki. Anderson," she nodded at Bill and escorted Caifen out the door. As they walked toward the parking lot, Caifen turned to look through the picture window and raised her hand in a wave to Buddy, a hopeful smile on her face.

CHAPTER 32

NINA SAT IN HER RENTAL car on the far side of the marina parking lot. She'd removed her wig and her shoulder length honey blonde hair was now cascading around her shoulders. She didn't want to risk removing the jacket, though she suspected her shoulder wound had stopped bleeding by now.

She watched as the CPS van drove into the lot, and Anderson waved down the woman who had arrived to take charge of Caifen. Nina scrutinized the woman through her binoculars. She looked tough, but had a kind face.

Nina stayed in her parking place until an hour later when the woman came back outside holding Caifen's hand. The little girl no longer looked terrified. Her posture was almost relaxed. While the CPS woman unlocked the van, Caifen took in her surroundings. Nina watched through the binoculars as the little girl's searching gaze swept the lot and found her. Nina lowered the binoculars and their eyes locked, just for a moment. The child acknowledged the woman who had saved her with a nod, and Nina's throat clenched. Then Caifen was lifted into the van, and driven away.

Nina continued to sit in her rental car, considering what had just happened. The only illumination in the large parking lot was from the street lights, and Nina's car was now in a dark corner, not where she'd parked when they'd arrived. How had the child known she was there? Nina was tired, and her shoulder throbbed, but what she'd seen in Caifen's eyes made everything she was doing worthwhile. Perhaps they shared a bond greater than most humans ever experienced.

Before she could think too deeply about that bond, Nina started her engine and motored back to her hotel. There were still five names on her list.

Chapter 33

After Melinda and Caifen left, Bill and I locked up the office and walked Buddy out onto the lawn before going down to the boat. He watered a few shrubs, and then suddenly lifted his head at the sound of an engine catching on the far side of the parking lot. Bill and I followed his gaze and saw a beige sedan driving toward the street. When the car was out of sight we turned to face each other.

"You don't suppose," he began.

"No. She wouldn't risk waiting around just to make sure Caifen was taken care of. Would she?"

Bill shook his head and yawned. "Let's get some sleep." He slung an arm around my shoulders and we strolled toward the locked gate. If I was lucky I'd get a couple hours of sleep before I had to be up again for my meeting with Brooke, and Stanley's funeral was this afternoon at 2:00.

Since Faulkner had Cross in custody, there was probably no further risk to Brooke, but the Archer issue remained. If Michael could get me his home address I planned to pay him a visit.

I was toweling off from my shower on Saturday morning when I heard the land line ring. Bill came into the head and handed me the phone, a quizzical look on his face.

"It's Michael," he said.

I smiled and took the phone, "Hey," I said. "Thanks for getting back to me."

I dropped my towel and went into the galley to find a notepad and pen. Bill grinned at my naked body wolfishly, but kept his hands to himself for the moment.

"I tried your office and your cell first," Michael said. "I've got that information you wanted."

"Of course you have," I laughed. Michael was amazing.

"Are you ready?"

I had the pen poised over the notepad. "Go," I said.

He read me an address in an affluent neighborhood in the Belmont Hills. Then, for good measure, he gave me Archer's social security and driver's license numbers.

"Wow. One of these days you're going to have to show me how you do that."

"I could, but then you wouldn't need me anymore. Good luck, Nikki. And be careful please, this guy is connected to some very unsavory characters."

"I will. Thank you, Michael."

I placed the receiver back in the galley charger and folded the page with Archer's information on it before Bill had a chance to read it.

"I need to get going," I said.

Bill was sitting at the galley counter sipping coffee. He just looked at me.

"Brooke's expecting me at nine," I said.

I was moving toward the stateroom when Bill's hand shot out and gripped my wrist. "Are you doing something that could get you hurt?" he asked.

"Not at the moment," I hedged.

"Remember our deal?"

I did remember. We'd agreed that I wouldn't keep secrets or lie to Bill about my work, and he wouldn't throw a fit when he didn't approve of my tactics.

"Yes, but I don't have time right now. I'll fill you in later."

"I'll hold you to that."

The wolfish grin returned to his face as he looked me over in a way that nearly changed my mind about my obligation to my client. Before my hormones could get the best of me I scooted into the stateroom and got dressed for the day.

"Hey," I called out while zipping up my boots. "Can you feed Buddy and take him for a walk?"

"Maybe."

"You don't have to work today, do you?"

"I have two open cases, but we both know who the killer is. I'll take care of your dog if you'll meet with an artist so we can get an identikit drawing of Nina's current face."

"Deal."

I rushed through my usual grooming routine, kissed man and dog, and sprinted up to shore.

When I arrived at Brooke's complex I found Jim, Robbyn, and Brooke all drinking coffee in the parking lot. Robbyn was telling Jim about life in North Carolina, and Brooke was looking radiant and slightly amused by her cousin's antics. Jim, who is a redhead, was blushing visibly, probably because Robbyn was standing very close, and Robbyn is very lovely. He looked up and spotted me approaching. His look said, "Thank God you're here." His lips said, "Morning, Nikki."

"Good morning, Jim."

Robbyn turned to me with a grin. "We thought our protector might need some coffee," she said, and laid a hand on Jim's arm.

He looked uncomfortable, so I decided to put him out of his misery. After all, he was doing this job as a favor to me.

"I'll take it from here," I said. "You go get some sleep."

"Good idea." Jim nodded, handed his empty cup to Robbyn, perhaps to give her something else to do with her hands, and said, "Ladies," before ducking into the white Mazda Protégé—one among many in his fleet of non-descript cars.

"Let's go inside," I said. "Can I get some of that coffee? I only had time for one cup and I didn't get to sleep until five this morning."

"Oh, poor baby," Robbyn crooned. "Did that detective of yours keep you awake, or was it work related?"

"It's a long story."

We slogged up the stairs—well, I slogged. Brooke and Robbyn pranced. Damned energetic Southerners.

While Brooke poured me a cup of caffeine I set about telling them what Cross had said during his interview and explained that I'd had a friend, who would remain nameless, get me a home address for Archer.

"I think you're safe now that Cross is in custody, and since you hired me to find out who killed Stanley, I need to take a closer look at Archer."

"Did Detective Faulkner say anything about when I can have Stanley's orchid back?"

"No, but since it's evidence, it might be a while. Why don't you give him a call? At the very least he might grant you visitation so you can make sure it has sufficient light, water, and whatever else orchids need."

"I have no idea what orchids need," Brooke said.

"Look it up online. Then call Faulkner. I have a feeling he'll be happy to hear from you. If you two can stay inside this morning, I'd like to take a drive and check out Archer's home. I'll meet you back here before the funeral."

"Do you want us to come with you?" Robbyn asked.

"Nope. Thanks, though. Please just stay put until I get back."

"How long do you think you'll be?" Brooke asked. "We were going to go to Aglaia for lunch."

"Have you made a reservation?"

"Not yet."

"Make it for three people at twelve o'clock. I love Greek food."

Brooke nodded, and I left.

I started the Bimmer, cranked up the air, and pulled my notes from my conversation with Michael out of the pocket of my slacks. Using my smartphone's GPS to locate the address, I hit the road.

Chapter 34

Archer lived on Belmont Canyon Road. I followed the GPS directions until I found the street, and felt a chill as I made the final right hand turn. The street was crowded with police cars, an ambulance, and what I assumed was a coroner's van. I pulled to the curb and parked.

I quickly scanned my smartphone, found Faulkner's number, and hit send.

"What is it, Nikki?"

"I'm at Archer's home address in Belmont and there are emergency vehicles everywhere. What's going on?"

"Shit. How the hell did you get this address?"

"So you're here?"

"I'm in the house. Stay in your car.

I'll be out in a few minutes," he said, and disconnected.

I rolled down the car windows and lit a cigarette. Fifteen really long minutes later Faulkner appeared striding down the long driveway through the gate and approached my car. As he walked he withdrew a cigar from his jacket pocket and lit up. I opened my car door to get out, but he held up his hand, indicating I should stay put. He walked around to the passenger side of the car and climbed in beside me, leaving the door ajar.

"We never had this conversation," he began.

"Okay."

"Tell me what you know about Nina Jezek."

"That's going to take a lot of time. I assume you've spoken with Bill this morning." Faulkner nodded. "So you know that Nina brought a child to my office around three a.m."

Another nod. "Anderson said you've agreed to help with an identikit rendering."

My turn to nod. I had no idea when I'd have time for that little chore.

"What exactly would you like to know about Nina?" I asked.

"Prior to this morning, when was the last time you saw her?"

"December. She killed a guy in Los Altos and I caught her coming out of his house. Maybe caught is the wrong word. I held her at gunpoint and she still managed to taser me. Nina is very resourceful."

"Uh huh. How would you characterize your relationship?"

"We don't have a relationship. Before that night in Los Altos I'd only met her once."

"Then why she would chose to bring an endangered child to your office."

"I asked her that very question."

"And what did she say?"

"She said, and I quote, 'I couldn't very well take her to the police, now could I?' And then she said she had to leave, and I shouldn't try to stop her."

"Did you?"

"Did I what?"

"Try to stop her."

"Oh, well, kind of. I pulled a gun on her, but she's HIV positive and was standing near the little girl."

"So rather than risk exposing the child to HIV, you let her walk out the door?"

"More or less."

"Shit."

"My feelings exactly. So what's going on at Archer's house? Why all the emergency vehicles?"

"Archer is dead. Killed sometime last night or early this morning. I came here to question him and found the security gates open and the front door unlocked. No one answered when I rang the bell, so I called for back up and went in with a couple of uniforms. Found him in the bedroom."

"Let me guess," I said, putting the final pieces together. "Knife wound?" Archer had never been married and had needed large sums of money to supplement his income as a CFO, probably so he could purchase kidnapped orphans to molest.

"Nope. Gunshot wound to the head. Close range."

"Wait. That doesn't make sense. You're thinking Nina killed him, right?"

"Yep."

"But she always kills with a knife."

"There was blood on the floor near the bed. Coroner says it's not Archer's."

"Ah. So Archer shot Nina." That explained the oversized, heavy jacket she had been wearing. She had to cover the wound to avoid getting her blood on Caifen.

"Looks that way. There are taser burns

on his chest, but he still could have gotten off a shot. The gun is registered to him. We also found a room where the little girl was apparently held captive." He shuddered as he thought about that. Faulkner was a good guy.

"If she's wounded she might seek medical attention."

"We're checking hospitals. It wasn't a lot of blood. Probably a flesh wound."

"Huh."

"What?"

"Well, she came here to kill Archer. He shot her before she could finish the job. Then, with a bullet wound, she took the time to bring the little girl to my office."

"What's your point?"

"I kind of admire her, to tell you the truth."

"The woman's a psycho, Hunter. A cold-blooded killer."

"A cold-blooded killer wouldn't have bothered to take care of an abused child."

Faulkner shook his head. "I gotta get back in there. I'm hoping Archer's gun will be a ballistic match to the weapon used to kill Godard."

"Will you let me know?"

"Sure. I have nothing better to do

than keep you posted on the status of all my investigations."

"Don't get snarky with me, Faulkner. By the way, your face is looking better."

He rubbed his jaw and shook his head again.

"Brooke wants to know when she can have Stanley's orchid back," I said, knowing it would annoy him further.

"It's evidence."

"It's a one of a kind hybrid. It needs special care."

"You are a pain in my ass, Hunter."

"So you've said."

"I'll talk to the DA and call Brooke about the orchid."

"You do that. We'll be having lunch at Aglaia at twelve, if you'd like to join us."

His eyes momentarily brightened, then he got out of my car and walked back toward the house.

Chapter 35

I called Bill on my way to Brooke's condo.

"Anderson."

"It's me. I'm going to be with Brooke until after the funeral. Are you okay with that?"

"You mean am I willing to stay with your dog so you don't have to feel guilty about leaving him alone on the boat?"

"Yeah. That's exactly what I mean."

"It's fine, but we need to get an identikit drawing of Nina circulating ASAP."

"I know. I can do that around four, if you want to set it up. It would help if we had a photo of Nina to use as a starting place. Then I can just tell the artist what's changed about her features."

"I'll see what I can do."

I heard Buddy chuff in the background and knew he was asking for a walk.

"Buddy needs a walk," I said.

"I'll call you back when I've set things up with the department."

He hung up before I could thank him for taking care of my dog, again.

Robbyn, Brooke and I drove to the restaurant together so I could fill them in on what had happened to Archer. It wasn't the kind of conversation you could have over lunch.

Brooke asked again about Stanley's orchid, and I said Faulkner would be calling to let her know. I didn't mention that I'd invited him to lunch because it seemed unlikely he'd take me up on that invitation, what with Archer's murder and all.

I parked the Bimmer in a public lot, and we crossed the street to Aglaia. I'd forgotten they had patio seating and felt a twinge of guilt knowing I could have brought my dog with me after all. I decided I'd over-order so I could bring him a nice box of leftovers after the funeral.

We started lunch with an order of Hummus and Babaganush into which we dipped fresh, warm, pita bread. *Heavenly.* The waiter offered Retsina, but we opted for water since it was too early in the day for a Retsina buzz.

I ordered the Greek Salad with a broiled chicken breast on the side, and Robbyn requested the Veggie Musakka. Brooke selected the Salmon Wrap. We were just finishing the appetizers when Faulkner strode up to our table, a huge grin on his face. He was carrying Stanley's orchid, a green ribbon tied around the glazed yellow pot. He bowed with a flourish and said, "Mind if I join you?" his attention clearly on Brooke.

Brooke blushed prettily, and I scooted over to the chair next to Robbyn who was now covering her smile with her napkin. Faulkner took the chair I'd vacated and gently set the orchid on the table in front of Brooke.

The look on her face was priceless. Her mouth was open, eyes sparkling, but no words were coming out. Suddenly she threw her napkin on the table and lunged at Faulkner, wrapping her arms around him. A bemused look crossed his face until he caught me and Robbyn openly staring at him. Then he patted Brooke on the back and leaned away from her.

She dug a tissue out of her clutch, wiped her eyes, and said, "Thank you so much."

Faulkner reached for some pita bread

and dipped it in what was left of the Hummus. "Not a problem," he said. "Once we found the gun that was used to shoot out Sutherland's tire in Cross's van, we had enough to hold him. There was also a Dell laptop in the van that we think was taken from Stanley's house. We might need the orchid if we go to trial, but it's yours until then."

Brooke beamed at Faulkner as the waiter set our entrées before us.

"Monday is the last day of the Santa Barbara orchid show," Brooke said, excitedly. "I can drive down tomorrow! This would have made Stanley so happy." She began to tear up, and Robbyn handed her another tissue.

Faulkner, uncomfortable with Brooke's tears, turned to me. "Archer's gun was a match." He didn't need to tell me a match to what. He was obviously being sensitive to Brooke's feelings, not mentioning Stanley's murder.

So, I thought, *Archer killed Stanley to keep him quiet about the embezzling, and Nina killed Archer because he was an active pedophile. What are the odds?* Not only were my two cases related, but one had resolved the other.

The four of us drove to Stanley's funeral together in Faulkner's Chevy. Brooke carried the orchid with her to the front of the room, and placed it on a table holding Stanley's urn and an enlarged copy of the photo of Stanley she kept in her wallet. I doubted that life sized depiction of himself had been part of Stanley's plan for today. I was glad to see that Brooke was doing what she thought was appropriate, instead of following her deceased beau's instructions to the letter. Stanley's orchid was now sporting a fully open silver-blue bloom, and outshone all the orchid plants the florist had delivered.

Brooke smiled sadly at Stanley's photo, then turned to face the small crowd which included some of Stanley's clients. I recognized the drycleaner, José Castillo, and the owner of the body shop, Scott Kopelin. It was easy to see the resemblance between Stanley and his family. His parents and siblings all had the same dark good looks, but their eyes lacked the tenderness that was visible in Stanley's photo. My guess was that Brooke had taken that picture, and Stanley had been gazing at her when she did.

All who were present were dry-eyed except Brooke. She withdrew a small stack of index cards from her pocket and began to read the eulogy Stanley had written about himself. When she replaced the cards in her pocket, her eyes rose to take in the group in front of her.

"I doubt Stanley would approve of what I'm about to say, but he was one of the warmest, kindest, and most eccentric people I've ever known. He struggled every day with the need to maintain order and balance, and that made him a brilliant CPA. Life wasn't easy for Stanley, but his expertise in his field made life easier for his clients, and for that we're all grateful." She turned to look at the photo and said, "I'll miss you, Stanley. Thank you for being a part of my life." She choked up on the last words, then took her seat between Robbyn and Faulkner. Faulkner reached for her hand and gave it a gentle squeeze.

The owner of the mortuary approached the altar and asked if anyone else would like to speak. There was some uncomfortable rustling in the small crowd, but no one volunteered, not even Stanley's family.

When the service ended, Faulkner, Robbyn, Brooke and I made the short drive to the cemetery where Brooke had reserved a niche in the Columbarium for Stanley's urn.

She'd had the niche engraved with beautiful silver-blue orchids.

On the way back to the parking lot I took her arm and slowed my pace so that Robbyn and Faulkner could move on ahead of us.

"There's something you should know," I said softly. "We've identified Stanley's killer."

Brooke gasped and covered her mouth with her hand. "Who was it?" she whispered.

"It was Geoffrey Archer. The gun that killed Stanley was found in his home."

"Has he been arrested?" she asked. "Is he in jail?"

"Not exactly," I said. "He was murdered in his home last night, or early this morning."

Brooke just stared at me, her mouth open, for a long time. Then she glanced quickly to where Robbyn and Faulkner were waiting, turned her back to them, and said, "Nikki... you didn't..."

"No," I smiled. "It wasn't me. I take my job seriously, but not that seriously."

"So who killed him? Do you know?"

"Actually I do. Her name is Nina Jezek."

"Why?"

"That's a story for another time."

Brooke nodded as though she understood, and we rejoined Robbyn and Faulkner at the car. Faulkner was unlocking the passenger door when Brooke reached for his hand. He dropped his keys on the ground and looked at where their hands were joined.

"I don't suppose you have time for a road trip," she said.

Faulkner's already burned face turned crimson. He cleared his throat, then said, "I might be able to take a couple of days off."

Brooke smiled happily. "That would be wonderful," she said. "Would you mind telling me your first name?"

"Oh, man," said Faulkner. "What the hell. It's Elton. My mom was a fan."

"I think it's a lovely name," Brooke said. Then she leaned in and kissed him.

What can I say? I'm a sucker for a happy ending.

-THE END-

About the Author

Nancy Skopin is a native of California, and currently lives on the Oregon coast with her husband and their dogs.

While researching her mystery series she spent two years working for a private investigator learning the intricacies of the business. She lived aboard her yacht in the San Francisco Bay Area for thirteen years, as does her central character, Nicoli Hunter.

Nancy also works closely with a retired police detective who is both a consultant and a friend.

If you'd like to be notified when new Nikki Hunter mysteries come out, email me at: NikkiMaxineHunter@gmail.com

Made in the USA
San Bernardino, CA
23 March 2016